Corey's Catch

~ West Series ~
Corey & Bella
© 2014 Jill Sanders

Follow Jill online at:
Jill@JillSanders.com
http://JillSanders.com
Jill on Twitter
Jill on Facebook
Sign up for Jill's Newsletter

Summary

Corey has dug himself into a hole so deep, he can't see a way out. His only goal now is to see this rough patch through. But then Bella Thompson waltzes into his life and knocks him on his ass—figuratively and literally. Now, there's nothing he wouldn't do to prove to her that his wild days are a thing of the past.

Bella isn't sure why she's chosen to stay in the small town of Fairplay, Texas, after her aunt's funeral. But she's never been one to back out of a situation. And after running into one of the sexiest and most headstrong cowboys she's ever met, she doesn't plan to start now.

Corey's Catch

by

Jill Sanders

Jill Sanders

Chapter One

Corey stood on the front porch of his old man's cabin and frowned as the police car drove away. It wasn't the first time his old man had been hauled off, nor did he figure, would it be the last.

Half the time anymore, he worked to pay the legal expenses from his old man's troubles. His dad, who seemed to only be getting crazier as he got older, had been taken down to the station more than a dozen times in the past six months.

As it was, he'd had to sell his newer truck to pay his lawyer, Grant Holton. Shaking his head and leaning against the post, he wondered how much this trip would end up costing him.

Wes Tanner, one of Fairplay's sheriffs, had hinted that maybe it was time to stop fighting and let his dad go into a state facility.

"There are places for people like him," Wes had said, wiping the sweat from his brow with a bandanna.

"People like him?" He'd been confused.

"Your dad's getting up there in years. You know…" Wes had leaned on the railing of the deck. "Some people lose their minds a bit the older they get."

"Like Mrs. Nolan?" He'd felt anger kick him in the gut, hard and swift.

"Hell." Wes shook his head. "I don't think your dad would do anything that drastic."

"No, but you're suggesting it." He'd pushed off from the porch and had stood his ground.

Wes shrugged. "He did just shoot your neighbor's dog with rock-salt pellets for peeing on his truck's tire."

Corey sighed and relaxed a bit. "Yeah, I'll be heading into town to see how much the vet bill will be." He shook his head and seriously thought about buying some flowers for old Mrs. Thompson. After all, the dog was the old lady's best friend. Actually, Corey had really liked Dutch, the woman's albino mutt. Dutch was only in their yard because Corey had been feeding it scraps while the older lady was laid up with the flu. During the past month, he'd also been helping her out with her other animals and her ranch, which bordered his father's property.

Kicking the door open, he stormed in to change out of the bloody clothes and into a dress shirt and dress pants he kept at the place. He knew he had a busy day ahead of him, kissing ass and paying for his father's bad temper.

One of the stops on his list was to Mrs. Thompson's place to let her know that Dutch had been taken into the vet with his hindquarters bloody and full of rock-salt pellets.

Corey was thankful that he'd changed out the shotgun shells in the old man's gun a few weeks back. Otherwise, the dog could have been seriously hurt and his father would be looking at bigger charges.

His heartstrings tugged when he remembered how Dutch had looked up at him as he'd helped carry him to the back of Chase Graham's truck. Chase was the local vet, and he'd assured Corey that Dutch would be fine and most likely ready to go home by the following day.

Still, he knew that he couldn't afford a vet bill on top of the lawyer bill he knew was coming, along with the bail money he'd have to come up with. Maybe it would be cheaper for him to have his dad hauled away and locked up. At least he couldn't get his hands on a gun again.

After showering and driving into town, he stood in the lobby of Grant's office and waited for the bomb to drop. His next stop would be the vet clinic, but for now, he needed to see if his father could get out on bail and what exactly the charges would be.

"Corey." Grant opened the door and motioned for him to go in. "I just got off the phone with the courthouse." He shut the door behind him and motioned for Corey to take a seat.

"And?" He wiped his sweaty palms on his dress jeans.

Grant shook his head. "Looks like they want to ship him to Tyler this time."

"What?" He almost jumped out of his chair. "What for? It was just rock salt."

Grant sat down behind his desk and nodded. "And the dozenth time he's been seen before the judge in five months."

"Six," he mumbled, resting back.

Grant looked over at him from his computer screen. "Four and a half, actually. I know his record is pretty clean up until just before New Year's and we talked about his health issues. But I can't help but wonder if there is something else going on. Have you two been getting along okay?" Grant leaned closer.

"Sure." He shrugged. "He's just getting moody. Like all people his age do."

Grant shook his head. "Most elderly don't go from model citizens to this." He pointed to the large file with his father's name on it.

"What do you suggest I do? Leave him in the pen?"

Grant leaned back in his chair and shook his head. "What about going with the plea of insanity?"

They'd talked about this a few times. The option, at this point, was looking better than it had a few weeks ago. After the trial, and if convicted, his father would be sent to a state facility a few towns away. The one where Travis' mother still lived. Looking across the table at the man who'd been shot by the woman made him remember just how crazy his friend's mother had been. Was his dad really heading down the same path? Could he really afford for the next incident to be a person instead of a dog?

Nodding his head, he kept his eyes glued to his hands. "I guess there's no other option at this point. I can't always keep an eye on him. Not with the work I've been doing anyway."

He'd been doing odd jobs around town to help pay for his father's bills for the past two years. Several times, he'd thought about leaving town and heading into Houston, but each time, his father had done something stupid like this to stop him.

"I'll make the necessary arrangements," Grant said, typing on his computer. "I know my brother-in-law is expecting you in his office. He's told me that Dutch should be ready to go home tomorrow. He's tried to get a hold of Mrs. Thompson but

9

hasn't been able to reach her on the phone."

He nodded. "She's almost deaf at this point. I was going to stop by and talk to Chase and then head over to her place myself." He stood up and shook Grant's hand. "Thanks for… everything."

Grant nodded as he shook his hand firmly. "I know things have been hard around the place."

Corey knew where the conversation was going. Grant was a good man and had on several occasions tried to convince him that he didn't need payment. "I'll cut you a check by the end of the month."

"Corey, don't put yourself in any financial trouble to—"

Corey stopped him by holding up his hand. "I pay my debts. We've talked about this. You'll have a check by the end of the month."

Grant sighed and nodded quickly. Corey turned and walked out as he mentally calculated his finances.

He'd been working with the West brothers for the last few months. Ryan and Reece had gone into business together. The newly settled Fairplay brothers had started a horse breaking and training business together. They had over a dozen colts and broncs they were working at the moment.

Corey worked on the ranch four days a week, which helped pay the utilities at his dad's place and his rent at the small apartment he rented from

Travis in town.

The way things were going, he figured he'd have to temporarily move out to his father's cabin, since it was paid off, to consolidate his own bills, which would save him a little under a thousand dollars a month.

He walked across the street to the clinic. The bell chimed overhead as he walked into the loud, sterile room. Several townspeople sat in the chairs along the windows, holding their various pets as they waiting for their chance to see the doctor. He walked up to the counter and asked to see Chase and was shown to the back room almost immediately.

"How's Dutch doing?" He shook the man's hand when he entered.

"Good. He did lose a chunk of his thigh, but he'll have no problems walking." He waved him back to a long room lined with cages and stopped in front of one. Dutch was asleep, his leg wrapped tight with gauze. There was a cone on the poor dog's neck. "He'll have to wear that for a while and there are meds he'll need to take." He turned to him. "I haven't been able to get a hold of Betty."

"I'm heading out there after I see Travis about something."

He nodded and started walking back towards the front. Corey followed him. When they got to the front, he turned and shook his hand once more.

"Dutch can be picked up anytime tomorrow."

"I'll see to it. I'll pay his bill tomorrow when I get him."

Chase dipped his head. "I'll have it ready for you." He turned to go. "Corey, for what it's worth, I don't think Mrs. Thompson will press charges."

"Thanks," he mumbled and then turned to walk out.

It was just a few blocks to where he knew he'd find Travis, so he strolled along the sidewalk.

The newly renovated bookstore and coffee house was pretty packed when he walked in a few minutes later. Instantly, he heard his friend's laugh and found him near the back corner, his face buried in his new wife's hair as she slapped at his shoulder.

"You two need to find a room instead of making the whole town sick by having to watch this gross display of affection," he joked as he sat in the seat across from them.

Instead of jumping apart, Travis just held onto Holly, the bookstore owner, even tighter.

"We were doing just fine where we were before you sat down." Travis looked over at him and frowned as he rested back against the booth, his arm still slung around Holly's shoulders. "We heard about what happened this morning."

"Course you did." He glanced around the shop

and noticed that several people were looking his way. "Everyone has by now." He'd lived in the small town his entire life and knew how everything worked.

Fairplay, Texas, didn't need a local paper to hear about what was going on. Not when there was Mama's Cafe and Holly's Bookstore and Coffee House.

"How's the dog?" Holly asked.

"He'll be ready to go home tomorrow."

"It's a good thing you replaced the shells with rock salt." Travis frowned down at his empty coffee mug.

He nodded, then waved to April, Holly's manager. She walked over with a cup of his favorite coffee and a blueberry muffin. He'd gone out with the blonde a few times, but then she'd met her new boyfriend. The pair was engaged to wed, which was how most of Corey's relationships had ended.

"Listen…" He looked to Travis. "I wanted to talk to you about the apartment."

Holly leaned over and kissed Travis' cheek. "I'll leave you two alone. I have some things I have to see to anyway." She stood up and smiled down at him. "I hope everything turns out okay, Corey."

Nodding, he took a sip of his coffee.

"So," Travis said, leaning back. "What's up?"

He took a deep cleansing breath. "I'm going to move out to the cabin for a while. Until things are square with the old man."

Travis nodded his head as he took a sip of his coffee. "Sure, we both knew this was coming sooner or later."

He felt his shoulders relax. "I know the lease isn't…"

Travis leaned forward. "Don't worry about the lease. There's a clause in there for emergencies. This applies."

He nodded, looking down at his cup. "Thanks."

"Don't mention it. Do you need any help? You know, moving. Or with the old man?"

Corey shook his head, still not meeting his friend's eyes. "No, I've got it." He finally looked up. "Sounds like they're going to move him to Conifer." Travis' mother was serving twenty at the same facility his dad would be at.

Travis' eyes met his. "How long?"

He shrugged. "The judge will see him later this month."

"Maybe it's for the best." Travis leaned forward. "My mother can't harm anyone else. She actually thinks she's on vacation." He leaned back.

"My dad…" He shook his head and took another sip of his coffee to try and soothe his throat. Then he laughed. "Yeah, I just don't see

14

that going well."

Travis tilted his head. "It's better than the alternative."

Corey knew what he was talking about. About how Travis' mother had almost killed a man and then had driven home to make fried chicken for her family as if nothing had happened.

He nodded and then looked up at him. "I'll have the place cleared out by the weekend."

"Take your time. If you need anything…"

Corey nodded and then stood up and tossed some money on the table to pay for his coffee and muffin, which he'd hardly touched. "Thanks."

Walking back to his old truck, he dreaded the next stop. Not that he didn't like Mrs. Thompson. Actually, just the opposite. The older woman had always been a part of his life. She'd been his longest running neighbor.

His father's father had owned the land and cabin. When his mother had been alive, they had lived in town. Then after she'd died of cancer, his father had moved out to the cabin. Corey had lived there for a few years until he'd graduated. Then he'd spent a while moving around, living at friends' houses until finally he'd rented the apartment in town from Travis' father, which Travis had inherited upon his father's death last year.

As he drove out of town and headed back to the

cabin, he thought about moving out of town once more. Selling the cabin and land and getting the heck out of Dodge.

But he knew that running away from his problems wouldn't solve anything. Dust kicked up behind the truck as he flew down the dirt road towards Mrs. Thompson's larger place.

The woman had a dozen or more acres that housed two large barns and a house big enough for at least a dozen kids, even though she had never married or had children of her own. She had been an animal lover instead. There were dogs, cats, chickens, horses, and cattle. At one point, she'd had a few pigs and goats, but she'd sold those off, telling Corey she couldn't stand the smell.

He stopped his truck behind her new pickup and frowned when he noticed the front door wide open.

Mrs. Thompson was in her late sixties and very independent. The woman was a workhorse when it came to keeping up her land. But she'd been sick the last few weeks and he'd made a point to stop by a few times a week to check up on her.

He hadn't been by her place for a few days, and he was worried when he walked up to the porch. Instantly some of the dogs and cats rushed him, begging for attention and food.

"Mrs. Thompson?" he called out, swinging the front door open. It was dark in the house and he had to blink a few times to see clearly.

Sweat dripped down his back as he stepped into the living room. At first, his mind didn't register what he was seeing. There on the floor, surrounded by her beloved animals, was Mrs. Thompson, her eyes wide open, staring up at the ceiling, unseeing.

Chapter Two

 ella stopped her small car at the end of the
drive and rested her head back against the
headrest. There was no way her Miata would make
it down the drive. Climbing out, she groaned when
her three-inch heels sank in the rich Texas soil.

Swatting a few bugs away from her face, she
walked around the small car and leaned into the
trunk to get her bags. She was so occupied with
thoughts of how she was going to carry the heavy
bags down the road, she didn't hear the truck pull

up behind her.

She had just pulled one of the heavy bags towards the edge of the trunk when she heard a voice directly behind her.

"Car problems?" The deep male voice shocked her and she spun around quickly. Her arms flung wide as she turned.

When the back of her hand hit something solid, she pulled her arms closer to her chest as she watched a very tall man lose his balance and fall backwards until he sat in the dirt. He looked up at her as he held his jaw.

"Didn't mean to scare you," he said, wiggling his jaw a few times.

"Oh! I'm so sorry." She leaned back on the trunk of her car, horrified that she'd almost knocked the man out. "Are you alright?" She held a hand out to help him up.

He glanced down at it and then dropped his hand away from his face and smiled up at her.

She gasped again, this time from the sheer shock of how sexy the man was. Even sitting in the dirt with a growing bruise on his chin, he was dripping sexuality.

She blinked a few times as she watched him stand up, without her help. She was thankful that he'd been too busy getting up to notice her second gasp.

"No harm done." He stood next to her and she had to crane her neck to look up into his blue eyes. He was wearing a long-sleeved button-up shirt and an old pair of jeans. His tan boots had a light dusting of dirt on them and they looked well worn. He'd removed his hat and was holding it in his hands when her eyes moved back up to his. He had sandy blond hair with a slight curl; the color matched the stubble on his face.

"I suppose you're Mrs. Thompson's niece." He tapped his hat to his thigh. When she nodded, he continued. "I'm real sorry about your aunt. She was a sweet lady." He glanced down at his hat, like he didn't know what else to say.

"Thank you, Mr...."

His eyes moved to hers. "Corey."

She arched her brows. "Mr. Corey?"

He chuckled, showing her the most perfect dimples on a man's face she'd ever seen.

"Corey Park."

She nodded. "Thank you, Corey," she said, turning back to her bags and trying to hide her flushed face. Those dimples were sending signals through her body that she didn't want to think about.

"I didn't catch your name?" he said, walking up to the edge of her trunk, close enough that his shoulders brushed up against hers.

21

She glanced over at him. "Bella."

He smiled again and she quickly looked away. Damn. If the man kept looking at her like that, she was going to have a hard time staying focused on building a new life. Men were trouble. At least that's all they'd given her in the past.

"Car problems?" He repeated his initial question.

"Hmm? she questioned. "Oh, no. I'm just realizing I should have rented a truck." She chuckled nervously.

"You can park your car here for now." He nodded to a spot under a large oak. "I can carry you and your luggage up to your aunt's in my truck."

She glanced over at his truck and wondered why she hadn't heard him pull up. She could still see dust settling from his wheels.

"That would be very kind of you." She reached in to grab her bag, only to have his hand rest on her elbow.

"I'll get those," he said, causing her to step back, out of his reach. "Why don't you park first."

He stood back as she pulled into the low grass. When she reached to open the door, he was already pulling it open for her and holding his hand out for her to take.

"Thank you," she said, letting his warm hand

pull her out of the small car. She held her breath when she realized how close he was to her. Then he took a step back and started walking towards her open trunk.

She stood back as he pulled her two bags from the trunk like they weighed nothing. He tossed them over the bed of his truck and then held open the passenger door for her.

She reached in and pulled out her purse and smaller bag and then made sure to lock her car up before moving over towards his truck.

"I've been watching your aunt's animals for the past few weeks. Since…"

She knew her aunt Betty had always been an animal lover. The last time Bella had visited, when she was twelve, the woman had had everything from chickens to pigs.

Instantly, worry flashed in her mind. How did one go about selling farm animals?

"How many animals?" she asked, leaning forward and looking at the place as they pulled closer to it. It was bigger than she remembered.

The house was painted a very light yellow with white trim. There was a large porch that wrapped around half of the house. White pickets hung from the top of the overhang, matching the railing of the porch. The roof was dark and looked brand new. All of the bushes and trees around the house were very well maintained.

"Your aunt really enjoyed working with all different kinds of animals. Rescued most of them. She had a real talent for yard work too. I've tried to keep it up since her passing," Corey said, stopping the truck beside a light blue Ford truck. "That's Chase." He pointed towards the barn as a tall, dark-haired man started walking towards them. When he saw the truck, he waved and smiled. "He's the local vet and has been helping out with the animals."

Corey jumped out of the truck and rushed to help her down.

"Morning," Chase called over. "You must be Betty's niece."

"Bella," Corey added in.

Chase stopped right in front of them and held out his hand. "I'm Chase Graham."

"Nice to meet you." She shook the man's hand.

"Everyone's doing just fine. I had another look at Dutch and took the cone of shame off him," Chase said to Corey.

"Thanks." Corey frowned and looked down at his boots. "I'll just take your bags in for you." The man turned and rushed away. She watched for a moment, until he disappeared into the front door.

"What was wrong with Dutch? More important, who is Dutch?" She giggled nervously.

Chase stuck his hands in his pockets. "Dutch is

the pit bull mix that Corey's daddy shot with rock salt."

"Oh!" She blinked and looked towards the house. "Poor thing."

"Don't worry. The dog has eaten up all the attention Corey's been giving him. Actually, he's been staying across the way..." He nodded to the left of the house. Her eyes moved over and saw a small brown home behind a row of trees. "With Corey. The guy has been spoiling him rotten."

She felt a little unsettled knowing the sexy cowboy with dimples would be so close for the next few weeks.

Chase glanced down at her heels and skirt. "If you want to change into something more suitable, I'll show you around and go over the animals' schedules."

She nodded. "I'd appreciate it." She started walking towards the house.

"My wife, Lauren, would be happy to come out and help. We've got two little ones now, but she always can find time to help out."

"That would be wonderful. I'm not too sure on how to handle animals." She stopped on the porch, holding the screen door in her hand. "Actually, maybe we can talk about the possibility of selling off some of the animals."

He nodded. "We'll be here to help with whatever you need."

25

She smiled then opened the screen and almost bumped into Corey just inside the darker hallway.

"Oh!" She gasped as his hands moved to her shoulders to steady her.

"Sorry," he said at the same time. "It's so dark in here." He frowned and then dropped his arms. "Your aunt always kept the drapes closed." He walked over and pulled back the heavy curtains, letting the bright sunlight into the room.

Instantly, Bella could see dust flying around the room. "I suppose it was so she wouldn't have to dust so much."

He nodded. "Actually, she was having some vision problems lately. The sun had been hurting her eyes."

"We didn't know she'd been in such bad shape." She felt the need to explain why no one from her family had visited her in years.

Bella's parents had come and gone for the funeral. But Bella herself hadn't been able to tear away from her life until now, less than a week later.

Her favorite aunt had left everything, including the farm, to her. Her parents couldn't have been happier, since they didn't want to deal with what they deemed backwoods issues.

Bella, on the other hand, had been looking for a fresh start. Especially after the Hugh incident.

"I hope I didn't hurt you." She glanced up at his jaw and noticed that the redness had already disappeared.

He chuckled and moved back in front of her. "No, just bruised my pride. I haven't been knocked into the dirt by a woman before." He smiled, showing her those dimples again. "Well, at least not when I didn't deserve it." He winked.

"If you want, I can keep Dutch at my place. At least until his leg has healed up."

She nodded and glanced around. There were two cats currently rubbing themselves against Corey's leg, begging for attention. He leaned down and picked one of them up, scratching it under its chin. "This is Beggar." He let the cat brush its face against his. "He likes treats and will do anything for them." He glanced down at the darker cat on the floor, who was just sitting up, staring at him. "That's Snubs. He's too proud to stoop to begging. He'll just stare at you and annoy you until you cave."

She chuckled. "What about the dogs?" She nodded to the front door, where two big dogs looked in at them. She could hear Chase out there talking to them and smiled.

"Rascal and Rusty. They're brothers. Dutch was the newest to the family. Your aunt rescued him after the last storm. We'll show you around." He glanced at her skirt and blouse. Then his eyes moved to her heels.

"I was coming in to change." She smiled nervously.

He nodded. "I put your stuff in your room."

"I'll just head up." She felt a little sad knowing her aunt wouldn't be there.

He stood back, holding the cat, watching her walk up the wide staircase. She felt like she was on a catwalk. She could actually feel his eyes on her and the heat from his gaze singed her, setting her body on a slow burn.

***

Corey stepped outside and whistled. "Never saw that one coming," he said slowly as he remembered the exquisite view he'd had of Bella's backside as she'd leaned into her car earlier. How more than just her backswing had caused him to fall backwards and land on his ass. He rubbed his chin, not wanting to admit that Bella had knocked him out in more than one way.

"What?" Chase asked from the front porch swing, causing him to jump. He'd forgotten the man was still there.

Shaking his head, he walked over and leaned on the railing. "Didn't see Mrs. Thompson having a niece like her." He nodded towards the house.

Chase laughed. "What did you expect?" He shook his head. "No, don't answer that," he said, holding up his hand. Then he stopped the swing from swaying and leaned on his knees. "I just don't know how a city girl like her is going to take care of all of this." He motioned to the large farm around them.

"Damned if I know. Did you see those shoes?" He whistled again, remembering how sexy those legs had looked in the short skirt and spiky shoes.

"Lauren only wears those kind when I take her into the city."

"Looks like we'll need to check in on her more often than we thought," he said quickly as he heard her coming back down the stairs.

When she stepped out, he had to do a double take. He'd thought she'd looked good wearing her city clothes. But seeing her in a worn pair of tight jeans, tan boots, and a long-sleeved button-up blouse that fit her tighter than the blouse she'd, been wearing earlier made his mouth go dry. She looked like a Texan, born to sit in a saddle.

"Ready?" Chase asked, getting up from the swing.

"Lead the way," Bella said, not even glancing his direction. It was a good thing, too, because he was sure that his chin was still down and his mouth wide open like he was trying to catch flies.

He leaned against the railing as Chase and Bella disappeared into the barn. He could hear Chase talking the entire time. He knew there wasn't a good reason for him to stick around much longer, but since he had nothing else to do for a few hours, he figured he'd see if she needed anything before he headed back into town and his next job.

The past few weeks, since they'd hauled his dad away, had been filled with nothing but work. He'd taken as many odd jobs as he could to help pay for the bills he was faced with.

Since Mrs. Thompson hadn't been around to press charges, the county had stepped in. Because of his dad's growing record in such a short time, they'd held him for evaluation. Apparently, it hadn't gone well since his father was now sitting at a state facility a county over waiting for his day in court.

He supposed that his father getting into a punching match with two county guards hadn't helped his cause. Especially since one of those guards had been the judge's nephew and had required several stitches.

He walked over and sat down in the swing. There was still so much that he would have to take care of before heading into work that evening. Besides working at the West brother's ranch, he'd taken on a few odd jobs painting houses and building decks. His back and arms had never hurt so much in his life. But the pay was helping cover the vet bill for Dutch, who he'd grown even closer to over the last few weeks.

Actually, he was slowly becoming inseparable from the funny-looking dog. Dutch seemed to enjoy having all the attention.

He looked down at Rascal and Rusty, who had initially followed Chase and Bella out to the barn but had quickly returned and were now lying at his feet, fast asleep.

Actually, he'd grown very close to all of the animals on the property over the last few days.

"So, remember, if you need any help…" Chase was saying as the pair stepped out of the barn.

"I'll call," Bella said, smiling up at his friend.

"Corey is just a holler away." Chase nodded towards him. Corey stood up and walked to the edge of the porch. "I'll leave my cell number for you." He smiled down at Bella.

"Here's my card. My numbers are all on there." Chase handed her a business card. "Well, I've got to get back to the office." He tipped his hat and started walking away, then turned back to her. "I'm sure you'll be seeing my wife and her sisters soon. Not to mention a few other ladies in town. They'll hear that you're here and want to stop by."

Bella nodded as she tucked his card into the back pocket of her jeans.

"Thanks, I look forward to meeting them."

They were silent for a while as they watched Chase's truck bounce down the drive.

"Does that mean you'll be staying on?" he asked when the dust had settled.

She turned to him, her eyebrows up in question.

31

"I haven't decided yet." She moved up the stairs and stopped just outside the door, still looking at him.

"So, you don't plan on selling then?" He shoved his hands into his pockets and leaned back on the railing.

She sighed. "I haven't decided yet," she repeated as she looked around the place.

He thought about it for a moment. "If you do, let me know first." He felt his heart kick.

Her eyes moved to his. "Are you interested in buying this place?"

He chuckled. "Since I was five."

She slowly smiled. "Fair enough, I guess, since your property borders this one." She glanced off towards his small cabin."

"It's not mine yet." He frowned as he followed her gaze.

"Oh?" She turned back towards him.

His eyes burned when he saw the small building he was currently living in. "My father still has a hold on it." His eyes found hers. "He might just take it all to the grave. He's stubborn like that." He mumbled the last part.

"I hadn't expected all of this." She glanced around again.

"Do you like living in the country?" he asked,

wanting to know more about her.

She shrugged her shoulders. "I have never lived anywhere other than the city."

He couldn't stop the laugh from leaving his lips. The fact was, he couldn't imagine living anywhere other than the country. He'd spent a while in the city and hated everything about it. The traffic, the noise, the smells. Everything. Then he watched heat flood her eyes and he regretted the move.

"Sorry." He shook his head.

"What?" She crossed her arms over her chest and glared at him. "You don't think I can make it?"

He shook his head. "I never—"

"My parents said the same thing." She huffed. "I don't need to prove anything to them or to you." She turned to open the screen door, but he was beside her in a flash, holding the door shut over her shoulder.

"That's not what I meant," he said in a low voice. "I have no doubt you can handle anything this place will throw at you," he said to her back. "The fact is..." He sighed softly. "I can't imagine myself anywhere other than here." He looked down at his hand over hers. His fingers were tan, calloused, and rough from hard work. Hers were pale, soft, and small. Yet he knew that any woman determined enough could accomplish anything and something told him that Bella was one of those women who would rise to the challenge.

When she turned around, he dropped his hand from hers.

"I'm sorry," she said, not really looking at him. Instead, her eyes were on his hands, which he quickly tucked back into his jeans. "I shouldn't jump to conclusions," she said, lifting her chin until their eyes met again. "Thank you for the ride and bringing my luggage in."

He nodded, not knowing what to say. Especially since his throat had gone bone dry from the sad look in her eyes. He didn't know what had really caused her outburst, but he was determined to prove to her that he believed in her.

"You can park your car at my place until you decide. The cabin is closer to the road and our drive is smooth." She nodded, looking up at him, her eyes glued to his. "If you need anything, just yell." He felt like someone had kicked him in the chest. His breathing was labored and he was having a hard time focusing his eyes on anything other than her face.

He took a step back, needing the space. Then, when she still just looked up at him, he turned and started walking back to the cabin.

"Corey," she called out to him.

When he turned around, he finally took a large breath as he looked at her. Her long hair was flowing around her face as the wind blew it over her shoulders.

"Thanks again." She smiled and waved.

He nodded, then turned and rushed back across the tree line where he felt his system level back out.

Chapter Three

That evening Bella was wondering why she had even questioned selling the large place. The kitchen sink, when turned on, sprayed water all over her shirt, soaking it. Only two of the oven's burners worked. The microwave made a funny noise, so she avoided using it all together.

When she'd gone upstairs to take a hot shower before crawling into bed, she'd quickly realized that there was no hot water. None.

It was sticky enough that the cold shower worked, but she knew there was no way she was spending a winter without soaking in a hot bath. She lay awake for a while until finally the cats crawled up in bed with her. The two dogs lay on their beds near the foot of the bed. One bed sat empty and she wondered what Dutch, the missing dog, would think when he returned home to find his master gone.

The sounds of an older house and the country surrounding it caused her sleep to be light. Finally, when the sun streamed in the window, she pushed out of bed and looked down at the two cutest faces she could ever remember seeing.

Rascal and Rusty both had their heads resting on the bed, looking up at her.

"What?" she asked, trying to hold in a chuckle. "Is it bathroom time?"

The dogs immediately started dancing around in circles. "Okay." She laughed as she pulled on her robe. "I'm hurrying." She almost tripped over one of them as they raced with her down the stairs. When she opened the front doors, they bolted outside and quickly disappeared around the edge of the house.

Walking out, she took a deep breath and smiled. It was very beautiful here. Going to the edge of the porch, she watched as a few chickens rushed from the side of the house. Rascal and Rusty were quickly on their heels.

Flying down the stairs, she tried to grab the dog's collars before any damage could be done. The dogs, for their part, thought it all a joke and made her chase them around the yard, circling the clucking chickens.

Feathers were flying as she cursed and yelled at the dogs to obey her. By the time she got a hold of one of the dog's collars, she was laughing so hard, her sides hurt.

"I've got you, Rascal. Rusty..." She glared at the other dog, who stood a few feet away, smiling at her. "You'd better come over here." She snapped her finger just as she heard a chuckle behind her.

When she gasped and spun around, her bare feet twisted in the soft dirt, causing her to lose her balance. She landed hard on her butt in the dirt just as Rascal bolted from her grasp.

Corey stood a few feet away from her, laughing.

"Don't just stand there. Grab those dogs before they kill all of the chickens." She moved to get up, but stopped when Corey continued to stand over her laughing.

Putting her hands on her hips, she frowned up at him and gave him her best glare. Of course, the fact that she was sitting in the dirt in her canary yellow robe probably didn't help the situation.

Once Corey was done laughing, he moved closer to her and pretended to wipe a tear from his eyes. "Best show I've seen all year." He helped her up by putting his hands under her arms and hoisting her up to her feet quickly.

Her short robe flew up so she reached down to hold it in place. Then she realized the left shoulder had fallen down and tried to put everything back in place.

"I hope you know that if those dogs destroy any

of those chickens…"

"They won't." He smiled down at her.

She frowned. "How do you know?"

He reached up and moved the right shoulder of her robe back into place. "They grew up around them. See." He stepped back and nodded to the yard. Both dogs were chasing the chickens, but instead of viciously tearing into them, it appeared that they were corralling them. "See. They're taking them to the field there, where they will roam free for a few hours. Then Rusty will lie down and watch over them until it's time to put them back up for the evening."

"What about Rascal?"

Corey turned back to her. "He's too selfish to waste his day watching over a bunch of hens." He chuckled and nodded to where the dog was running around the yard, smelling and peeing on everything.

"What are you doing here?" Her brain finally clicked into gear enough to ask him as she started walking towards the house to get dressed.

"I was letting the chickens out." He started following her back up to the porch.

"Now that I know they need to be let out, I can do it." She glanced at him as she walked. He was already dressed for the day in old jeans, a tight T-shirt, and work boots. He looked like he was ready to hop on a horse and hit the trail.

"It's no problem," he smiled at her as he pulled a basket out from behind his back. She hadn't even known he was holding anything.

"I see." She chuckled. "You sashay over here every morning and let the hens out while you steal their eggs?"

He nodded and then held out the basket for her. "But, now that you're here…."

She peeked into the basket and looked up at him. "What would I do with over a dozen eggs every morning?"

He grinned. "Eat them of course."

"A dozen?" she asked as she climbed the stairs.

"Why not?" He almost ran into the back of her when she stopped suddenly. When she turned around, she had to crane her neck to look up at him. Instead of answering him, she reached into the basket and pulled out three eggs.

"The rest you can have." She started to turn and then stopped. "If you want to let the chickens out every morning, feel free." She smiled and then turned to go inside. She was a little shocked to hear him follow her inside.

Heading to the kitchen, she glanced around and pulled down the black pan from the rack.

"Why don't you let me do this so you can go up and change?" He set the basket on the counter and took the pan from her.

41

She narrowed her eyes at him.

"What's in it for you?"

He grinned, showing her those dimples again. He'd shaved this morning, making him look even sexier without the stubble that he'd had the day before.

"Free breakfast with a beautiful woman."

She decided to stop herself from crossing her arms over her chest. Instead, she thought about fighting with the burners on the stove and nodded. She turned and went upstairs as the cats made their way towards the sounds in the kitchen.

"I see you two are finally up," she said to them as they passed her on the stairs. Beggar gave her a meow as he passed but then rushed to the sound of a can being opened in the kitchen. Snubs slowly walked by her with his tail and chin up in the air.

It was funny how quickly she was picking up the personalities of the animals. She wondered if she would be able to do that with the other animals around her aunt's place.

She jumped in and out of the shower in record time. Not just because it was frigid, but because she had started to smell wonderful things coming from the kitchen below.

She had made herself comfortable in her aunt's room. It was the largest room and had the most comfortable four-poster king-size bed. The high ceiling was vaulted, pointing up to a spiky A with huge windows that overlooked the back of the property. This morning she could see all the way to the back fields where the tree line started. The mist had hung in the air, making the whole field glow with the morning sun.

There weren't any curtains over the high windows, which had been one of the reasons she'd woken so early. But since she'd always been a morning person, she didn't mind.

Pulling her wet long hair up in a tight braid, she walked downstairs to hear Corey chatting with the cats.

"Snubs, why can't you be more like your brother here? I mean, Beggar will do anything for this." She heard him chuckle and walked in to see the cat climbing his leg for a piece of cheese.

"Doesn't that hurt?" she asked, leaning against the door frame.

He glanced over and shook his head. "Not really. He's really quite gentle. He learned a long time ago that if he hurts me with his claws, he doesn't get the treats." He gave the begging cat the cheese and dropped a piece for Snubs.

"It smells wonderful." She glanced over at the plate of bacon and bowl full of scrambled eggs.

"I hope you like spicy." He walked over and set the bowl down and she realized there were onions and tomatoes in the eggs.

"Love it," she said absentmindedly as she took

a deep breath and enjoyed the spices opening all of her senses.

She sat down as he set a plate in front of her.

"If you want, I can swing by later this week and have a look at the burners for you. Two of them aren't lighting up."

She leaned back. "I'd rather know why there isn't any hot water."

He sat down next to her. "I can check that as well." He pushed the bowl of eggs towards her.

"Can you really eat ten eggs yourself?" she asked, scooping some onto her plate.

"Sure can. Especially when I know I won't get time for lunch today."

"Oh?" she asked, handing him the bowl. "Why is that?"

He took it and started scooping eggs onto his plate. "I'm working with the West brothers today. We're trying to break Hellion."

She just looked at him and shook her head lightly.

"Sorry, Hellion is a stallion we've been trying to break. You know, so we can ride him."

"I understand the concept." She chuckled as she took a piece of bacon and nibbled on it. It was perfection. Actually, the eggs were even better. Everything tasted so fresh. "So, is that what you do full time? Break horses?"

He shrugged his shoulders as he took another bite. "Sometimes."

She waited, but when it seemed like he wasn't going to continue, she asked, "What else do you do?"

He looked up at her. A little irritation crossed his blue eyes. "This and that around town."

"Like a handy man?" When he nodded, she added. "It appears there are some things that need to be done around here." She looked around the kitchen. She'd started making a list last night and knew there was probably more she would find over the next few weeks. Her eyes went back to his and she realized he'd been watching her. "If you're handy with power tools and can fix the stove, you're hired."

He thought about it for a moment. "I'll swing by early tomorrow."

She smiled as she shoved another piece of bacon in her mouth.

"If you need any help today," he said a few minutes later as she followed him out to the front porch, "just let Chase know."

"Thanks for breakfast," she said, holding the screen door open.

"Thank you for the eggs." He winked and then turned to walk back to his place.

She watched him for a moment, enjoying the way his tight jeans fit. It had been a long time since she'd seen a man fill out a pair of Levi's so well.

Her chores outside took her most of the morning and, she had to admit, had worn her out plenty. She'd been a little cautious with some of the bigger animals at first, especially the cattle. They had very long horns and images of being impaled flashed through her mind.

But after cleaning out the outside stalls and filling their trough with fresh water, she realized that they were too lazy or hot to really bother with her.

The horses were something completely different. Here she spent time with each one. Her aunt had four all together. Two smaller ponies and two full-size quarter horses. Ollie was older and looked like he was struggling to keep up with the others as they moved around the penned yard.

The younger quarter horse's name was Lizzie. She was gray and had such a fun personality. Bella had been surprised to see a large blue ball in the pen with the animals and stopped when Lizzie started playing with the thing like a dog.

She leaned against the post and laughed as she and the two ponies, Kasper and Yogi, tried to keep the ball from Lizzie. Ollie just stood back and watched the show.

By lunchtime, she was thinking about enjoying one of those cold showers since she was covered in sweat and a thin layer of hay dust.

It was nice that all of her outside chores were taken care off and all of the animals seemed to be happy. She used the rest of the day to move around inside, making more lists of things Corey could check or fix. She had a small amount in her savings and had planned on using it to fix the place up. After all, even if she did decide to sell the old house, these items would have to be done before it could be put on the market.

Since she didn't have any plans currently to go back to the city and her dead-end life, she was happy to continue where she was for a while. The thought of having a sexy cowboy around fixing up the place didn't hurt either.

Chapter Four

It was one of those days that started out really great and then went to hell in a hand-basket. Corey was used to being thrown from a horse, but being stomped on afterwards was something new to him.

Every inch of his body ached as he hobbled up the stairs of the cabin. Hellion had certainly earned his nickname that day. Thoughts of soaking his body in a hot bath crossed his mind. When he opened the door, Dutch hobbled over, asking to go out.

He leaned against the railing while the dog did his business. His eyes kept moving over to the lights across the field. All day long he'd been distracted with thoughts of Bella—what she was doing, how she was adjusting to life in the country. Most important—would she stick around?

Fairplay, Texas, was a small town. Not a lot of people moved to the middle of nowhere where there were few possibilities of great jobs or lives.

He knew there was a good chance that Bella wouldn't want to stick it out. Especially because Mrs. Thompson's place had gotten so run down over the past few years. Just the thought of helping Bella out made him wish he could avoid the rest of his work. Especially working with Hellion.

He groaned when he finally slid down into the steamy tub. Dutch watched him from a comfortable spot on the floor. He had to be honest with himself—the dog was healed enough to go home. It was Corey that needed him to stick around.

He must have fallen asleep in the bath because the next thing he knew, the water was freezing. Pulling himself out and wrapping a towel around his waist, he walked into the kitchen to grab a beer just as there was a soft knock on his door.

Dutch let out a loud bark and ran to the door. He slid on the hardwood floor and banged his head solidly on the door. Chuckling at the stupid mutt, he flipped open the door and smiled at Bella, who was standing outside in the soft porch light.

"Hey," he said, leaning against the door frame.

"Hey." Her eyes moved over him, making him realize he was still in just a towel. "I didn't mean to bother…"

He waved her in as he opened the screen door.

"No bother. I'll just go toss on some clothes. Dutch can keep you entertained for a minute." He motioned to the dog who was now lying down, drooling at their feet.

"Oh." She squatted down and scratched Dutch's head. "Okay." She giggled when the dog promptly flipped over and asked for a belly rub.

He walked back into his bedroom and tossed on a clean pair of jeans and grabbed a shirt. She looked good. Real good. She'd changed out of her work clothes and was wearing jean shorts and a pale yellow tank top. Just seeing those legs again made his heart rate spike.

When he walked out, she was standing in the middle of his living room, looking around.

"Pardon the mess. I'm still trying to get settled in." He walked to the kitchen and pulled out a beer. "Want one?" he asked.

She shook her head no as she tucked her hands into her pockets.

He popped the top and took a deep drink.

"Long day?" she asked, and he smiled.

"That horse was out to kill me today." He leaned against the counter and looked at her. "You

51

look like you enjoyed your first day on the farm."

Her lips dipped up in a smile, causing him to focus on how soft they looked.

"I can understand why my aunt loved it here."

He watched her fiddle with her fingers and then tuck her hands back inside her pockets.

"Bella, did you need something?" He watched her eyes move around and then finally land on his.

"I was wondering…" He waited as she took a deep breath. "I hate to ask…" She paused again.

"Just spit it out." He smiled over at her.

"It's just that I was really hoping for a hot bath." He watched her roll her shoulders and felt like laughing when the thought of her joining his bath flashed through his mind.

"I'll just slip on some boots." He set his beer down and started walking towards the door. He could feel her following him and when he held open the front door, Dutch started to walk out.

"Is he up for the trip?" she asked, frowning down at the dog.

Chuckling, he answered, "Dutch has made a full recovery. He's just gotten used to sticking around here." He glanced up at her. "If you want, I can keep him around for a while. Until you decide…"

She smiled. "Corey, if you want the dog, he's yours. Besides, it looks like he's already made himself at home around here." She nodded to the dog bed and the basket full of toys he'd bought for Dutch.

He stopped her from walking outside. "Really?" His hand rested on hers, keeping her in front of him.

"Corey, I'm not one hundred percent sure I'm not going to find new homes for all of the animals my aunt has." She sighed. "At least not yet."

He nodded. "You'll let me know first. I have a few I'm rather fond of."

She glanced down at his hand on her arm, so he dropped it and shoved it in his jean pocket.

"You'll be the first to know." She stepped outside and Dutch followed. "Actually, I was thinking of calling Chase."

"Is there a problem with one of the animals?" he asked as concern built.

"No, not that I'm aware of. I just wanted to know how old Ollie was."

He laughed. "As old as the hills. That horse was old when I was born."

Her eyebrows shot up in question as she glanced his way. He stopped to hold a tree branch aside for her to pass under. The pathway was fairly dark, but there was enough light from the stars and moon that they could see clearly.

"Well, okay, not really, but it seems like it.

53

There hasn't been a time when I didn't think that he was old. Maybe he has just always acted old." He thought about it for a moment. "My uncle had a dog once; I swear Calvin never acted like a puppy." He smiled.

"You like animals." The statement kind of threw him off.

"Who doesn't?" he asked as they walked into the clearing. All of the lights were on in the big house. "Afraid of the dark?" he joked.

She glanced up at the house and frowned. "I'm not used to living in such a large place."

When they got closer, Rascal and Rusty rushed out to greet Dutch.

"They get along great," Bella said, smiling as the dogs rushed around the yard, barking and playing.

"Yeah, it's one of the reasons your aunt brought Dutch in for good. Even Snubs likes him." He walked up to the door and tried to open it and laughed again when it was locked. "Honey, you're in the country now. We don't lock our doors."

She frowned up at him as she pulled out her key and unlocked the deadbolt. "Something else I guess I'll have to get used to."

He walked into the back kitchen, opened the utility room door, and flipped on the light. Instantly, the smell of gas made him take a step back. "Damn," he said under his breath.

"Problem?" she asked from right behind him.

"Yeah, smells like you have a leak." He walked over and opened the back window and then turned and pulled her out of the room. "We'll call the gas company from outside. Grab Beggar. I'll get Snubs."

"Is it that bad?" She frowned as she followed him.

He nodded as he snatched up the grumpy cat, who looked at him like he was crazy. "You never want to mess around with gas." He held the door open and waited until she walked out with Beggar in her hands.

He set the cat down, and he instantly jumped up on his spot on the front swing and started bathing himself. Pulling out his phone, Corey hit speed dial to the police station.

When Cathy, one of the dispatchers answered, he knew what should be a short conversation would end up taking longer.

"Hey, Cathy, I'm over here at Mrs. Thompson's place with Bella—"

"Oh, is that her niece? I heard she'd come into town. Haven't seen her myself yet," the older woman broke in. "Course, everyone in town is talking about how pretty the girl is."

"Yeah." He sighed and crossed his arms over his chest. "Well, she has a gas leak…"

"Oh, you get those animals out and I'll send over Roy." He could hear her punching her keys on the keyboard.

"Yeah, everyone's out. We'll just wait—"

"You should bring that girl in to Mama's. Have her meet everyone properly."

"Will do."

"I swear, that man is slower than dirt. Hang on Corey. I've got to call Roy on the other line."

"Cathy, we'll just wait—" But it was no use; the woman had put him on hold. Rolling his eyes, he turned and smiled down at Bella. "She's getting Roy, who works for the gas company."

Bella nodded and leaned back against the railing.

"She says I should take you into town to Mama's Diner. Everyone wants to meet you."

"Oh?" she asked, frowning a bit. "I'm not—"

But Cathy broke in and he had to hold up a finger to stop Bella.

"Well, he says he's on the way. Course he was upset that I broke into his game. But that man always has a game he's watching anyway." She chuckled. "Now, where was I? Oh, yeah, Mama's been going on how no one visits anymore. Especially you, Corey. You've been so busy rushing around since your pa was taken in, that you don't have a lot of time for socializing." She sighed. "Boy your age ought to have a woman on your arm. A good woman. Don't you agree?" she added and he felt the hit land solidly.

He'd been seen around town the last few years with a lot of different women. Women he'd found out at bars in Tyler. None of them had stuck around longer than a few weeks.

"Yes, ma'am." He nodded and tried to figure out the quickest way off the phone. "Well, I'd better go. Bella's standing right here," he added, winking at her as she looked at him questioningly.

"Oh, yes. You go on and chitchat with that girl. You make sure to ask her out now. Give me a call if you need anything else tonight."

"Will do. Thanks Cathy." He hung up and released a sigh. "Sorry, I kind of threw you under the bus there."

She just looked at him, and her eyebrows went up.

"Cathy will talk your ear off." He walked over and sat next to the cat. Beggar jumped up onto his lap and he started scratching the cat under his chin.

"How did you throw me under the bus?" she asked, walking over to sit next to him.

"I sort of agreed that I'd take you into town for dinner."

She turned to look at him as Snubs jumped up on her lap. He was a little shocked, since the cat had never even let him pet him. He must have looked shocked, because she frowned at him.

"Are you okay?"

"How did you do that?" he asked, pointing to the cat. She was now petting the cat and Snubs actually looked like he was enjoying it.

"What?" She looked down at the cat.

"He's never so much as let anyone pet him before. Not even your aunt. You practically have him purring." He stopped and leaned closer. Sure enough, there was a light purr coming from the cat. "Amazing." He leaned back and shook his head.

She chuckled. "I guess he's just picky who he loves."

Corey thought about it for a moment. He thought about all of the women he'd dated over the years. Then he looked up into Bella's blue eyes and said,

"I feel exactly the same way."

***

Bella stood back and watched Roy, an older gentleman in green overalls, show her how to light the water heater pilot. He'd spent the first twenty minutes sealing off the small leak she had under the heater.

When he told her it was a good thing the pilot had gone out before the leak occurred, she was determined to make replacing the tank first on her list. Roy filled her in on what it would take to replace the tank and suggested she go with a tankless water heater instead. He told her if she had one, she could have a hot bath within minutes.

"It'll take this tank about two hours to get warm enough for a bath. You might be best to wait until morning." He wiped the sweat from his forehead with a bandanna.

She hid a groan. Her muscles were screaming at her from mucking out the stalls. But at least she wasn't in danger of blowing herself up tonight.

"Two of the burners aren't working right," Corey broke in, nodding to the stove.

"Is that right? This old thing needed to be replaced years ago. I told your aunt that many times." Roy walked over with his toolbox and started working on the burners. "They're all mucked up," he said as he worked.

"I'm looking into buying a new stove," she said to his back.

"Good. This thing isn't safe. Your aunt always spent her money on those animals instead of making this place safe." He shook his head as he banged a piece of pipe on the countertop. "Muck," he said again, shaking his head even more.

Corey chuckled. "Roy, can you get it cleaned or not?"

Roy looked over at him. "Course I can." He banged on the piece again. "See." He held it up and then spent the next few minutes cleaning the other piece. By the time he was done, all four burners lit up. "Like I said, you'll want to replace this and the heater soon."

"Thank you." She shook the man's hand. "If you'll send me the bill…"

"No need." Roy took out the bandanna and wiped his hands on it. "I owed your aunt a visit anyhow. I should have had this checked long ago." He shook his head. "Betty was a classy lady. We're sure going to miss her around here."

"Thank you," she said again. She felt her eyes begin to water, so she turned and walked towards the front door. When she opened the screen door, both cats rushed in, followed more slowly by all three dogs.

Roy walked out, carrying his toolbox with him. "It was a pleasure meeting you. You let me know if there's anything else you need." He dipped his hat and disappeared into the night.

She sighed and leaned against the door frame and then jumped when Corey walked up behind her.

"That's how things are done in small towns." He brushed his hand down her shoulder. "You're welcome to come over and use my shower or tub if you want."

Just hearing the low invitation rumble from his chest had images flooding her mind. The memory of seeing him dripping wet, half-naked jumped into mind. She'd never seen a man so sexy before. He was all lean muscle. Tan and hard. She'd never dated a man who'd looked so... raw and rugged before.

"Thank you, but I think I'll just head up to bed." She shook the images of his sexy body out of her mind. It wouldn't do to get distracted. Sure, he was going out of his way to be extra nice to her, but in the end, relationships always ended the same. With bitter disappointment.

"Well, if you change your mind...." He opened the screen door. "Are you coming, Dutch?" He turned and waited.

The dog looked around and then walked slowly to the door and glanced back at his buddies.

"You can stay if you want," he said to the dog. But Dutch walked outside with his head high.

"Looks like you have a dog." She smiled and glanced down at the other two dogs, who were lying by the fireplace, watching their buddy leave.

"Yeah." He smiled, showing her those dimples. For a moment, she second-guessed her decision not to follow him home like the dog was. Then he turned and walked out. But before he stepped off her porch, he turned back. "How about dinner tomorrow night. I'll take you into town and show you around."

She thought about it and seeing no harm,

61

nodded.

"Great. Around seven?"

"I'll be here." She smiled. "Thanks for your help tonight."

He smiled. "I stood back and let a seventy-year-old man do all the work."

She laughed. "You dealt with Cathy."

"That's true." He waved, then turned and started walking home.

Flipping off the lights as she made her way upstairs, she decided that she was too tired for a bath anyway. Her muscles still hurt, but that wasn't the main reason she'd gone over to Corey's tonight anyway.

When she was lying in bed, staring up at the dark ceiling, she had to finally admit it to herself. She had just wanted to see him again.

Chapter Five

The next morning, Bella enjoyed her first hot shower in days. Afterwards, she felt so much better and was able to rush around outside doing her chores. Instead of staying inside after lunch, she decided to pull down a saddle and take Lizzie for a short ride.

Lizzie was so excited when Bella walked out of the barn with the saddle. The horse knew instantly she was going for a ride. Bella could already tell she was going to thoroughly enjoy the ride. It had been years since she'd saddled up a horse.

Lizzie stood patiently, waiting and watching, as she fiddled with the harness.

"Well, you can't blame me really," she told the horse as she finally got the buckle clipped. "It's been years since I went to riding school." She sighed as she leaned up and patted the horse. "Don't hold that against me though. My parents insisted on it."

She walked Lizzie over to the fence and, using the bottom rung, climbed into the saddle. "There." She smiled and leaned down to pet the horse. "Now we're ready." She kicked off and Lizzie bolted towards the open field.

Her hair flew away from her face in the cool wind. The speed felt wonderful. She'd forgotten how nice it was to sit on the back of a horse.

They rode to the end of the field where the fence cornered them in, and then she turned Lizzie and rode along the fence until they had gone all the way around the entire property.

Near the back of the property, there was a small pond near a row of pine trees. Pulling Lizzie to a stop, she decided to enjoy the shade for a few minutes as the horse took a drink from the water.

She sat with her back to the tree and thought about her choices. Go back to the city and try to find another dead-end job and an apartment that would cost too much for not enough space, and deal with her family and friend issues. Or stay here. Looking around she took in a deep breath. The air was fresh and there was only the buzzing of bees and the chirping of birds around her.

She was beginning to really enjoy the company

of the animals. Even though she hadn't made it into town yet, she could remember Fairplay from when she'd visited a few times. She remembered thinking that it was small and being disappointed that they didn't have a McDonald's or a Wendy's. In her youth, fast food had mattered a lot to her.

That and escaping her parent's wrath. Not that they had been mean. Just strict. Very strict. School was her one priority in life, according to them. When she'd finally begged to join a sport, her mother had signed her up for private riding lessons. She'd wanted to be around other kids her own age, but instead had spent hours on the back of a horse, alone.

She didn't mind, she thought as she looked over to where Lizzie was grazing on the tall grass. People were a bother. At least the handful of friends she'd had had turned out to be. Most of the girls she'd tried to be friends with had turned on her once she'd broken things off with Hugh.

Maybe it was the caliber of people she hung out with. After all, she'd only become friends with Jenny and Tiffany after she'd started dating Hugh. Come to think of it, most of her friends in the past had come by way of her dating someone.

Glancing at her watch, she figured she had better get back and get ready for her date with Corey. Just the thought of the word *date* made her pause. This wasn't a date. Not really. He was just showing her around town, taking her out for dinner and introducing her.

Gathering Lizzie's reigns, she jumped up on the horse's back and headed back towards the barn at fast speeds. Lizzie seemed to like taking it fast.

"I could become addicted to this," she said as she rubbed the horse down, cooling her off. Lizzie glanced at her and nodded her head like she understood. Bella laughed. "I could become addicted to you too." She rubbed the gray horse's mane. Lizzie used her chin to nudge Bella's shoulders closer. Laughing, she went in and hugged her. "Okay, I have to go or I'll be late. I don't want to be late meeting the town now, do I?"

Lizzie looked at her and shook her head. Bella was sure she was just swatting flies, but still it made her feel bonded with the animal to believe that she had answered instead.

She rushed through a quick shower and then stood in front of her suitcase and frowned. She didn't have anything that was appropriate for a not-date. What did one even wear for an occasion like this? Jeans?

Tossing her clothes around, she finally found a jean skirt that hit her just above her knees. But she couldn't find a top that looked right. Opening her aunt's closet, she found a white knit top and when she tried it on, it fit perfectly. Then she noticed a pair of her aunts black dress cowboy boots. When she tried them on, she jumped and dropped the boot when she felt something inside. Tipping the boot up, she gasped when a wad of hundreds dropped out.

Sitting down, she unwadded the roll and felt light-headed as she counted out almost ten thousand dollars. Holding her breath, she looked into the other boot but came up empty.

Still, ten thousand dollars would go a long way towards buying a new stove and water heater. Tucking the money back into a wad, she decided it would be best to shove it into another pair of her aunt's boots. Before she did, she checked all of the other shoes and came up empty again.

As she slid on the boots, she closed her eyes at the comfort and the gift her aunt had left. So much money hidden away that her aunt could have used. Why would the woman hide it away instead of buying herself a new stove or water heater?

When she heard the dogs bark downstairs, she knew Corey had arrived before she heard the knock. Rushing around, she gathered her purse and double-checked herself in the mirror one last time. She looked like a Texas girl. Her long blonde hair was left curly and tied back from her face in a loose braid. The knit shirt was beautiful and showed off her assets just right. Smiling, she did a little turn and decided the boots had been a perfect addition.

When she walked down the stairs, she smiled at Corey, who had let himself in and was loving both of the dogs. When he heard her walking down the stairs, he looked up and she watched his chin drop as he looked at her. His eyes ran slowly over her entire body. She noticed that he took a little extra time looking at her legs.

"Are you ready?" she asked in a breathy tone. The way he looked at her had taken all of the air out of her lungs.

***

Corey was thankful he was squatting down petting the dogs. Because just the sight of Bella made his knees go weak. She looked even sexier in the short skirt and cowboy boots than the spiky heels and tight skirt he'd first seen her in.

"Are you ready?" she purred with the sexiest voice he'd ever heard.

Now he was afraid of standing up because his dress jeans had gotten a little too tight all of a sudden. He had a moment of fear thinking that his voice would crack when he answered, so he just nodded instead.

She reached the bottom of the stairs and smiled down at him. "Well?"

He shook his head and tried to think of an extremely cold shower or anything so he could stand up without embarrassing himself.

Then he decided to try something different. After all, he wanted to make sure she understood his intentions. He quickly moved closer to her and took her shoulders with his hands. When he pulled her close, he watched her eyes go soft. "I just have to get this out of the way," he said, and then he laid his mouth over those sweet, soft lips of hers.

She tasted like sweet cherries. He couldn't seem to get enough. Especially when her fingers dug into his hair, holding him closer. She moved slightly, pushing her body up against his and he knew the moment she felt his desire. He held his breath, waiting to see how she would react.

When he felt her melt against him, he groaned and started to take a step towards the stairs. Then she pulled away.

"Wait," she said, putting her hand to her forehead and shaking her head slightly. "We... I... This is too fast," she said, glancing down at her hands.

"I'm sorry." He frowned as he watched the gold band around her wrist sparkle in the light. He was trying to cool himself down, but when he looked back up at her, he could still see the desire in her eyes. "I hadn't planned—"

"I know," she broke in. Then she smiled at him and he felt a little steadier.

"How about that dinner?" He held out his hand and smiled when she nodded and took it.

As they walked out, he chuckled when she turned and locked the door behind her.

"I know. I know." She sighed. "Old habits. But, it will make me feel better to keep it locked.

69

Besides, you'll never believe what I found tonight." She turned and took his hand again as they walked down the stairs.

"What? One of Betty's wads?" He laughed when her chin dropped.

"How did you know?"

He sighed. "Your aunt has been hiding cash since before you were born. Everyone in town assumes she has money stashed all over the place. I found some myself when I was helping her plant her garden a few years back." He laughed as he held the truck door open for her. "She told me she'd forgotten all about the sealed box of money she'd buried out back."

"Why didn't she use it to fix the place up?" she asked after he got behind the wheel and started pulling out of the drive.

He shrugged. "Not sure. She wouldn't tell me. Just said she was saving it up for later."

Bella looked down at her hands as he pulled out of the bumpy drive. "I guess later never came for her."

He reached over and took her hand as he drove. "Use the money how you see fit. If you want to fix the place up, I'll help." He glanced at her as he turned onto the main road into town.

"Thanks. I'd like to fix a few things. The drive probably should be top of the list since I doubt anyone without 4X4 could get down it."

"Most everyone in town has a 4X4," he joked. "Except city folk."

She sat quietly as he drove through the small town. He pointed out all the main attractions and realized that Fairplay didn't really have anything too exciting.

"That's the Rusty Rail. There's karaoke there every Thursday night. It's the only bar and place to dance in town." He nodded to the new coffee shop. "That's Holly's. If you're big into espressos and coffees, they have what you need." He pulled his truck in front of Mama's and stopped. "Here we are. The best place to eat in Texas." He glanced out the front window and smiled. "The place was damaged pretty bad a couple years back in that tornado we had." He shook his head, remembering the wreckage of the small town. "But Mama fixed it up right."

"Mama?" Bella asked, leaning forward to get a better view of the diner.

"Jamella, but everyone calls her Mama. You'll see why." He smiled and got out of the truck and rushed around to open her door.

After helping her down from the truck, he took her hand and walked slowly to the front door. When the bell chimed above them as they entered, several pairs of eyes turned towards them. All of a sudden, he felt more nervous than he had ever felt.

"There you are." Jamella rushed from behind

the counter and engulfed him in a big hug. The woman was short and very large, but knew how to give some of the best hugs ever. He closed his eyes and held on. "You been hiding yourself." She hummed as she stepped back and glared at him. "Ever since dat pa of yours got himself locked up." She put her hands on her hips and huffed as she shook her head.

"I'm sorry," he said, keeping his eyes locked on his feet. It was true; he'd been hiding from the town since that day. Sure, he was rushing around town, doing his work. But he'd avoided places like Mama's and the Grocery Stop since he didn't want to bump into anyone.

"Hmmm," she said and smiled. "I'll forgive you dis time." Then her eyes moved over to Bella. "Now, who'd dis pretty thing?"

He smiled. "Bella Thompson, this is Jamella."

"Thompson? Oh, sweetie. I'm so sorry to hear about your auntie." Jamella moved forward and wrapped her big arms around Bella, who, for the first few seconds, looked very uncomfortable. When she noticed him smiling at her, she relaxed into the hug.

"Thank you," Bella said once she was freed.

"Betty was a wonderful woman." Jamella motioned for them to sit in a booth near the front door. "She did love my apple pie."

"Mama, everyone loves your apple pies," Corey

said as he sat.

"Dat true." Jamella let out a loud and hardy laugh. "You two sit tight and look over dat." She handed them each a menu. "I'll be right back." She hustled off to deliver an order.

Before they could order, several people stopped by their booth on their way in or out of the diner. Everyone introduced themselves to Bella and conveyed their condolences.

One of the people to stop by was Ronny and his son Chris, who had been sitting in a back booth. Ronny walked up to them before they left Mama's and introduced himself to Bella while Chris paid their check.

"I was a dear friend of your aunt," Ronny said, using a handkerchief to wipe his nose. "I'll miss her very much." At that point, the old man cleared his throat and walked out without another word.

Several of the townspeople were very moved when they spoke about her aunt. Corey, too, felt sad that she was gone.

Finally, when Jamella came back to the table to take their orders, he felt like people would leave them alone. After ordering, a silence filled the booth. For the second time that night, he felt nervous.

"How long have you lived in Fairplay?" Bella asked, leaning closer to him.

"I was born and raised here. Most everyone

around here, it's the same story."

"You've never lived anywhere else?"

He shook his head. "Thought about it a few times, but the city just doesn't seem to be my thing. How about you?"

She leaned back and looked around. "For the most part, I grew up in Houston. We stayed there until my early teens, and then my parents moved around a lot. City to city. Until I moved out on my own, I was never in the same spot longer than a year or two. I was in Austin before I came here."

"Doing what?" He leaned back and tried to get as comfortable as he could in the small booth.

"This and that." She picked up her napkin and tried to focus on setting it in her lap just right. He could tell she was trying to avoid the question, but he wanted to know more.

"Did you go to school in Austin?" He crossed his arms over his chest and waited.

"Yes, some." His eyebrows shot up and he waited again. Finally, she sighed. "I dropped out of college." She shrugged. "I thought I had found the one."

"One? What?"

"The one. The man I was going to marry."

"And?" He felt his heart kick.

"And, he dumped me and married the woman

his parents wanted him to."

"Ouch." He looked into her eyes for any sign of hurt, but all he saw was anger and disappointment. "His loss."

She nodded, not letting her eyes meet his. "He took all of our friends with him. So when I heard that my aunt left me this place…" She shrugged and looked out the front windows at the small town.

"A fresh start," he added. When her eyes turned back to him and locked on, he felt like he could totally relate to how she felt. Except he hadn't moved hundreds of miles to start again.

"What about you?" she asked. When he tilted his head in question, she continued. "School? Relationships?"

"No college. No relationships that lasted more than a few weeks. Pretty boring stuff."

"What about your father? I've heard…"

He was thankful she was interrupted when their food was delivered. They started to eat, and he enjoyed the silence for a while. Then he decided she needed to know more about his old man and he set down his fork.

"My father's been going downhill for the last few months. The past year to be honest." He leaned back again and looked out the window at the small town that he felt comforted by. He knew the real reason he stayed was that he was too afraid to leave the support and friendships behind. "I've heard the words dementia and Alzheimer's more this year than I care to admit. The fact is, he's just plain gone off his rocker." He felt frustration building and turned back to her. "He was always an ornery cuss, but nothing like this. He'd never hurt an animal in his life. Well, except when we went hunting." He shrugged.

"What about your mother? Family?"

"My mom took off a few years back." He looked out the window again. "I haven't heard from her since."

"I'm sorry." She frowned and nibbled on a french fry.

"She was never really into living in Fairplay. She'd always dreamed of going to far-off places. I guess she's finally living her dream."

"Have you tried to contact her about your father?"

"No, I don't even know where she is." He wished for a beer, but knew that Mama didn't sell alcohol. Actually, since his old man had been hauled off, he'd slowed down on the drinking.

"What's going to happen to your father now?" she asked before taking another bite of her hamburger.

"He'll go before the judge in a few days. Then we'll find out."

"Do you have a lawyer?" she asked.

"Yeah." He nodded to the corner where Alex and Grant Holton sat with their two kids. "Grant's the town lawyer. He's pretty good. Studied up north. He's been helping out since the trouble started."

"If you need anything." She looked down and reached for his hand. "I dropped out of law school."

He jumped a little and looked up at her. "Seriously? You were going to be a lawyer?" He instantly felt not good enough for her. Why would a woman like her give a guy like him a chance?

She nodded and then dropped his hand. "But don't hold it against me." She chuckled, but he could see pain in her eyes and swore he'd get to the bottom of it.

Jill Sanders

Chapter Six

ella sat back in the truck as Corey drove her home. When they started up her bumpy lane, she turned to him.

"What do you think about riding lessons?"

He pulled behind her aunt's truck and flipped off the engine. "For kids?"

She nodded. "Yes, I took riding lessons when I was young. I've been thinking about it." She glanced around at the setup her aunt had. "With a few minor changes and a couple more reliable horses, I could start giving lessons."

He leaned back, his arm going behind her as he thought. His fingers touched her hair, and she felt like leaning her head back so he would play with the long strands.

"Little kids or bigger ones?"

She smiled. "Both."

"I might know a few horses that will fit just right. Course, Kasper and Yogi are good for smaller kids. Ollie is old enough and patient enough to let anyone ride him. Lizzie..." He shook his head and laughed. "She's too spirited."

She smiled and remembered her ride from the day. "I know. I took her out today. We had a blast." She started to get out of the truck and then watched him rush around to her side to help her down.

The dogs rushed over to them, barking and playing, and she leaned down to pet them both. She laughed when they jumped up and tried to kiss her.

"Down," Corey broke in. Both dogs obeyed quickly.

"You'll have to teach me how to do that," she said, laughing.

"Commanding them is easy; you just need to use a stern voice." He turned to the dogs. "Go on." He pointed to the house and both dogs raced towards the door.

"What else can they do?" she asked as she walked towards the house.

He chuckled. "That's pretty much it. I'm sure if

you have the patience and time, you could teach them more. Your aunt didn't really take the time to teach them much."

She walked over and sat on the swing, then patted the spot next to her. Corey smiled and sat next to her. His arm went around her shoulders again. This time his fingers did tangle in her hair.

"You're really thinking of sticking around here?" he asked and her mind swirled around the possibilities.

"I've been thinking about it. I mean, I don't see that there's anything left for me in Austin." She knew without a doubt that there was nothing left for her in that town. Nor did she want to chance running into anyone she knew there. They had made their choices and they'd chosen to drop her. Corey was right; it was their loss.

"What about your folks? Where are they now?"

"They moved to San Diego last year. I missed them when they were out here for my aunt's funeral."

He nodded. "I remember seeing them, but they didn't stick around here long."

"They never do." She leaned back into his shoulder and sighed. "I really like this place. Everyone seems so nice and helpful."

He chuckled, the sound reverberating against her ear. "That's because they are. You know, there was a time when I was younger that I couldn't stand being here. Everyone was too good." He pushed off, setting the swing moving slowly. "I did my best to show the town that I was just as bad as Billy and Travis, two of my buddies. The three of us raised so much dust in this town, it's still not settled."

She laughed and looked up at him. "I can see that about you." She watched his lips move up into a grin. Those dimples flashed and she felt her stomach jump. "What about now? Are you still a troublemaker?" she asked, feeling a little breathless.

He reached up and used his fingertips to push a strand of curls away from her face. "Not so much. Only in some areas." He leaned down and covered her lips with his again. This time the kiss was slow and when he took her deeper, she willingly went.

Her fingers dug into his scalp, pulling his thick hair closer as his mouth slanted over hers. His hands were traveling down her neck, slowly, until he pulled her shoulders closer to his chest.

She felt his heart beat next to hers and enjoyed the way his hands ran over her arms, her ribs, her hips. When the dogs whined, they both ignored the sound. Not until they heard one of them growl did they finally pull away from one another.

"What's wrong?" Corey asked, looking down at the dogs, who were both standing on the edge of the porch, the hair on their backs standing straight up.

"Easy," he said, standing up and moving towards them. "What's out there?" He moved to get off the porch when they heard a bang. Then he turned back to Bella. "Tell me you didn't leave the trash cans open."

She thought about it. "I'm not sure. Why?"

"Best get inside," he said, without answering her.

"Why?" She moved closer to him. "What is it?"

"Probably an opossum or raccoon, but just in case it's a black bear, go ahead and take the boys inside." He nodded to the two dogs, who were still growling.

"Bears? There are bears around here?" She glanced around, fear shooting through her quickly.

"If you leave your trash open, sure." He moved to step off the porch, and she raced over and grabbed his arm.

"You're not going out there!" She yanked on his arm until he stopped.

He laughed. "I've lived here my entire life. I can handle myself."

She shook her head. "No, come on in. We'll wait—"

"Bella, go, take the boys inside. I'll be right back. It's probably just a few raccoons."

Bella reached down and grabbed both of the

dogs' collars and had to practically drag them into the house. She turned on every light as she went around the place, looking out the windows and making sure the doors were locked. She knew it was stupid, but something made her want to check and make sure everything was in place while Corey was outside. She thought about opening the back door and checking on him, but just as she moved closer to the door, she heard him come in the front door.

"All clear. Looks like it was a few opossums. I've scared them off and closed your trash cans. You'll want to make sure you use the latch next time."

She nodded, feeling her heart rate slow a little. "I didn't know." Her hand was covering her heart.

"Don't worry about it." He walked up to her, taking her shoulders in his hands and pulling her closer. "I'm sure the opossums enjoyed the snacks." He smiled and kissed her forehead. "Well, I'd better get going. I've got an early morning."

She followed him back to the front door, feeling a little better that he'd scared the animal off for her. "Thank you for dinner." She held the door open for him, but he stopped in front of her instead of walking through.

"I have the weekend off. I can be here early to help around the place." He ran his hand down her arm and she felt the heat spread. What she wanted to do was invite him upstairs, but she knew it wouldn't be the right thing for her to enter into another relationship. At least not so soon after the whole mess with Hugh.

"I plan on going into Tyler this weekend and looking at some appliances. Maybe you'd like to go with me?"

"Count on it." He leaned down and placed a soft kiss on her lips. "Bella." His eyes met hers. "I like what's started between us. I plan on exploring it further."

She felt her knees go weak and was thankful she was leaning against the door. "Me too."

His smile was quick and those sexy dimples of his flashed, and then he turned and disappeared into the darkness.

Shutting and locking the door, she leaned against the wood and closed her eyes for a moment. Her body was vibrating from Corey's touch. No other man had made her feel this... wanted... special, before.

Even when she'd first met Hugh, the man that she'd assumed was everything she'd ever dreamed of, she'd never reacted to him the way she was now. As she made her way upstairs, the cats and dogs following her, she decided she needed to take things slow. Every relationship she'd ever had before, she'd jumped into quickly, and every single one had ended badly.

For some reason, this mattered more. Maybe

because she could see herself building a life here. Even if there were bears and opossum. After all, where else was she going to be handed the opportunity to start fresh in such a wonderful place.

***

Corey cussed up a storm as he flew through the air. He could hear Ryan and Reece laughing at him when he finally landed in the soft dirt of the corral.

"Shut up," he growled as he wiped the dirt from his face. "I'd like to see you do better." He glared over at the two matching faces.

"Is that a challenge?" Reece started to climb the rungs of the corral.

"Oh, no you don't little brother." Ryan, the older of the twins, grabbed Reece's pants and tugged until his boots hit the ground again. "If I let you back in there with that..."—Ryan nodded to Reece's arm, which was still in a cast from his fall a few weeks ago—"your wife will have my head." Missy, Reece's wife, worked at the local medical clinic in town. She was a spitfire and had given even Corey strict orders not to let her husband near Hellion for at least two months. "Not to mention our cousins will probably string both of us up." Lauren, Alex, and Haley were even more stubborn than Missy was. Just the thought of crossing any of the three ladies made him cringe.

Reece sighed and turned back to Corey. "If

you'd follow my instructions," Reece said, waving his good arm around, "you wouldn't end up in the dirt all the time."

"Not everyone can be an expert bronc rider like you." Corey leaned down and picked up his hat, then dusted it off on his jeans.

"That's right," Reece said, smiling big. "But, you've got some talent and besides, you're here." He nodded towards the black beast, rightfully nicknamed Hellion.

Reece had moved to Fairplay last year after retiring from the bronc busting circuit. The guy was a legend. His twin brother, Ryan, had been an undercover narcotic cop in Houston but had retired shortly after Reece had started his own business busting horses.

He'd been hired by the brothers to help out just a few months ago. At first, he'd really enjoyed the job. Now he absolutely loved it, even when he walked in the door at night, bruised and sore.

It paid better than painting walls and hammering, something he'd always loved doing, as well. There were a lot of odd jobs around town, and he had been making a name for himself as the go-to handy man. He'd spent a few hundred on his own tools and a lock box for the back of this truck to keep all of them in.

Thinking about his other job only made Bella pop back into mind.

"We've lost him again, bro," Ryan said, slapping Corey's shoulder. "That's the problem with him."

"What?" He turned on the two brothers.

"Women," they both said in unison.

"We heard you were out with the city girl last night," Reece said, smiling up at him.

"Mrs. Thompson's niece," Ryan added. "Heard she's a real looker."

"Don't let your wife hear you say that," Corey mumbled as he made his way back towards Hellion. He reached out for the horse's reins as Reece and Ryan continued to taunt him. He heard a truck drive up, but didn't dare take his eyes off the horse for a moment.

He was just about to jump on Hellion's back, when he heard Bella's voice behind him. His head spun around just as the horse leaned in and snapped his teeth around his wrist.

"Son of a..." He jumped back a few feet, but his foot was stuck in the stirrup, causing him to fall backwards and land on his ass once more.

He heard the brothers burst out laughing once more. He didn't know what was worse, the horse or the twins. When he looked over, he felt another kick to his chest. This time it was Bella that had caused it instead of Hellion.

Hobbling over to the gate, he walked out and

slammed it shut. "That's it. I'm calling it a day." He glared at the brothers and then turned to Bella, who was looking at him with concern. "What are you doing here?"

Chapter Seven

"Are you okay?" she asked, moving closer to him and taking his wrist in her hand. She tugged his glove off and pushed up his jacket to see the nasty bruise the black horse had given him.

"Yeah." He frowned down at her and she could tell that he was trying to shake the pain off. "What are you doing here?" he asked again.

"I'm checking out a horse. I heard about it from his cousin, Alexis, who stopped by for a visit this morning." She'd been pleasantly surprised by the woman's visit that morning. Alexis—Alex—had been very eager to fill Bella in on the town and everyone in it.

She had brought along some breakfast rolls and they had chatted over coffee for almost an hour

91

while her two kids, Laura and Gavin, played quietly with the dogs. That had eased her mind about whether Rascal and Rusty could be trusted around small children. Alex had assured her that they had visited her aunt plenty of times and that the only animal that ever had issues was Snubs, who just seemed to think children were to be avoided.

After she'd told Alex her plans of starting a riding school, Alex had told her about her cousin Reece, who might have a few horses for sale.

Being as eager as she was, she'd jumped in her aunt's truck and driven over shortly after Alex had left.

Corey stood back as the two attractive, identical men walked over to her. "Bella, this is Reece and Ryan," Corey introduced the brothers.

"Your cousin said you were thinking of selling a horse?" she said to Reece, the one with the broken arm. If he hadn't had the cast on, she doubted she would be able to tell them apart.

"I have a few older ones that have been rehabilitated." He nodded towards the barn. "If you want, you're welcome to take a look at them."

She felt excitement kick in at the possibility of having another horse that would fit in her plans.

"She's wanting them for riding lessons with kids," Corey added.

"Oh?" Ryan said as he followed them all into

the barn.

"Yes, I was thinking of teaching. I have my aunt's two ponies and Ollie," she explained.

"You'll want a solid horse. Your aunt's gray quarter horse is too spirited to put a kid on," Reece said, opening the barn door. "I should know. I trained her." He smiled.

"Lizzie. Yes, she's more my speed." Bella smiled.

"I've got Ralph here." Reece stopped in front of a stall that housed a beautiful red quarter horse. "He's been around the block a time or two, but he's half Ollie's age and is real gentle. I've been looking for a good home for him for a while," he said as he pet the horse's mane and leaned into his neck.

"I'd like to ride him, see how he handles." She waited.

"Sure thing." Reece patted the horse's mane and then turned to go.

"I'll saddle him up," Corey jumped in. "I can take King out and ride with her."

"Suit yourself." Reece relaxed. "You know where everything is." Reece slapped Corey on the back and turned back to Bella. "Let me know what you think of Ralph. He's about the only one I'm willing to part with right now."

"How long have you had him?" she asked as

Corey walked away to grab the gear.

"About a year. Found him out near the old abandoned silo a few miles out of town. No one seems to know where he came from."

She rubbed the horse's neck and watched his eyes roll back with enjoyment.

Corey got both horses saddled and ready for a ride while she talked with Reece and Ryan some more. In less than fifteen minutes, they were ready to go.

After jumping on Ralph's back, she turned to watch Corey hop up on a larger quarter horse's back. Corey's movements were smooth, like he'd been riding his entire life.

"You don't have to go with me," she said as they made their way out of the gate.

"Anything is better than dealing with Hellion." He nodded to the large black beast that was rushing around the smaller corral. "I swear he's glaring at me," he mumbled, causing her to chuckle.

"How's your wrist?" she asked, after they had made their way into the open fields behind Reece's place.

He glanced down at it and moved it back and forth. "It'll be stiff tonight, but at least it's not broken."

"Is that what happened to Reece's arm?" she

asked, enjoying the way the horse obeyed her slight commands.

"No, he took a dive off the roof when he was trying to patch it a few weeks back."

"I bet that hurt his pride a bit." She held back a laugh.

He glanced at her in question.

"Oh, come on. I'm not dead. I know who Reece West is. I have been to a rodeo once or twice in my life." She smiled. "I bet that man has broken more bones in his body than everyone in town put together."

He chuckled and nodded.

"Then he retires and breaks his wrist working on his own house." She smiled over at him, her eyebrows going up. "And has to hire someone to break his own horse."

He laughed. "When you put it like that, it is kind of funny."

"What does Ryan do?" she asked.

"He breaks horses too. Reece says he's not as good at it as I am. The two argue about it all the time."

"They seem like they enjoy working together." The old loneliness of not having a brother or sister resurfaced. She turned Ralph around and then pulled on his reins to back him up. The horse followed her lead perfectly. "I'd like to kick him into a run." She glanced at him. "Think you can keep up?" She smiled as she kicked the horse.

"Lead the way," she heard him say behind her. They made their way across the field quickly as she took the horse in a big U. By the time they were heading back towards the barn, she'd made up her mind about Ralph.

"So," he said, pulling up beside her. "How's he doing?"

"He's perfect." She smiled over at him.

Less than a half hour later, she was the new owner of Ralph and she felt like the decision was finally made. She was staying in Fairplay and starting her own riding school. There was still so much she had to do to get ready.

Now, besides working on the house, she had a corral to build and equipment to buy. She made a mental list as she drove into town to stock up on groceries.

Parking the truck in front of the Grocery Stop, she grabbed a cart and started down the first aisle. She was impressed that they were well stocked and found herself picking from the fresh produce with the thought of making Corey dinner. She loved to cook, something she'd taught herself after she'd moved out on her own.

Her mother had never been one to cook or bake and she found great joy in knowing she could create something her mother found too mundane to do for herself.

By the time her cart was full, she had talked to at least seven people in the store, most of them people who stopped her to express their thoughts about her aunt. It was funny, most people she hadn't met yet didn't even question who she was. It was like a bulletin had gone out throughout the town with her picture on it, stating who she was.

But she didn't mind. Actually, it was quite nice. Everyone introduced themselves and told her what they did. She'd met two teachers, a nurse from the clinic, and an auto mechanic's wife and her three girls, who showed great interest in taking riding lessons this fall. As she stood in the checkout line, she'd met Billy, Corey's friend, and his wife Savannah. The couple had recently married and had the most adorable dark-haired girl, Maggie.

"Corey has told me so much about you two." She smiled. "I mean three."

Savannah smiled. "Soon to be four." She rubbed her small belly.

"Congratulations." Instantly Bella felt a sense of emptiness that she'd never experienced before. She'd never once in the past few years thought about children. But with the big house sitting empty, the animals running around, suddenly the thought of kids didn't scare her as it had in the past.

"Thanks." Billy put his arm around Savannah's

shoulders. "We should have you and Corey over for dinner soon. He's been hiding himself from his friends ever since his father was hauled off."

She watched Savannah shiver and wondered why.

"If anyone knows how that feels, I do." Billy frowned and pulled Savannah closer.

"What do you say to coming out to my place next Friday? Corey was going to go into Tyler with me this weekend to help pick out some new appliances."

"Corey? Shopping for appliances." Billy chuckled. "Told you." He glanced down at his wife, who only smacked his stomach.

"Shut up," she growled lightly. "We'd love to come out. You let us know if we can bring something."

She nodded, as she started to unload her cart onto the belt as the young woman started ringing up the items.

"How's it going. You must be Bella. I'm Carmen, assistant manager here. If you need anything, just let me know. Did you find everything okay?" she asked as she scanned all her items quickly.

"Yes, I just love that you have a local produce section. Is this local honey?" She held up the glass bottle with the small label.

"Yes, actually, that's something new this year. The Walters are selling it along with some of Mrs. Walter's jams."

"The blueberry is the best," Savannah said from behind her, holding up a jar.

"I've always wanted to learn how to make jelly," she said out loud.

"I'm sure Karen will be happy to teach you. I can give you her number if you want."

"That would be wonderful," she said, thinking about all the grapevines along the back of the barn. Her aunt's small garden would be enough to keep her stocked up, not to mention all the eggs the chickens were producing every day. She had a basket full in the fridge and wondered if Corey would take even more off her hands each day.

"I was wondering, do you happen to know what my aunt did with all those eggs?"

"She gave them away at her church meetings. If you want, I can see if Ronny could stop by and start picking them up. Ronny helped your aunt out in the fields in exchange. He owns a mower and baler and bales her fields every fall. Then stacks the hay in the barn."

"All that for some eggs?"

Billy chuckled.

"What?" She turned towards him.

"Ronny was smitten with your aunt." Savannah

shoved her elbow into her husband's stomach once more.

"Oh." She felt a rush of sadness come over her. She'd never once thought about her aunt having a man.

On the trip home, she kept thinking about it. She didn't even know where the man lived. But she had told Carmen to tell him that he could stop by for the eggs. Hopefully, within the next few days, she would get to meet him.

When she drove up, the dogs were running around, happily chasing the truck. When she parked, she gave them attention before unloading the groceries.

She'd bought the biggest bag of dog food, the same kind she'd seen in the pantry. She'd even gotten a box of treats for them and the cats. As she unloaded the cans of cat food, Snubs and Beggar pushed against her legs, meowing like they hadn't been fed in days.

After feeding all of the animals, she started putting her own groceries away. She was standing on the stepladder, trying to put a big bag of rice away, when she noticed the box near the back of the pantry.

Pulling it out, she opened it and walked over to the table and sat down. More money was rolled up, but it was the small envelopes that stopped her. Envelopes with her childish handwriting on them.

Pulling out the worn paper, she opened one and pulled out the letter she'd sent her aunt years ago.

Dear Aunt Betty,

I can't thank you enough for the birthday card. I had a fun birthday party. I'm spending the money you sent me on a new riding helmet. My mother has enrolled me in classes and I start next week. I love wearing my riding outfit and got in trouble the other day when I wanted to wear it to school. I sure wish you could come visit us here in Boston. I don't like the cold and wish I was there on your big ranch in Texas.

Well, I have to go since my mom is making me write all the other people who gave me cards. I love and miss you so much. Give Bear a hug for me.

Love Bella

Tears streamed down her face as she read through all the other letters she'd written her aunt. Every single one was kept in the small box and it looked like they had been read over and over.

She'd never realized how much she had meant to her aunt. She wished she could have just a moment with her to express her own love once more. After all, the woman seemed to have loved her more than anyone else ever had.

Jill Sanders

Chapter Eight

There were a couple things Corey hated doing and shopping was one of those things. He enjoyed the nearly hour-long drive into Tyler with Bella sitting beside him, chatting about her first week in Fairplay.

But the second they hit the appliance store, he needed a beer. Ten minutes into shopping, he realized he'd lucked out since it appeared that Bella had done her homework.

It took her just a few minutes to pick out the tankless water heater, and less than ten to pick out a new stove and fridge. She even purchased a freezer for the mudroom.

"The freezer out there doesn't even work," she said as she shook her head. Then she turned to him

103

as the clerk was ringing her up. "I've found three more stashes,." she whispered. "Close to fifty thousand dollars. Where did my aunt get so much money?"

He shrugged. "No one really seemed to know. Some guessed that she was really a rich heiress." He waited and when Bella chuckled and shook her head, he continued. "Others thought she had a rich lover."

"I thought… That is, I was told that Ronny and her…"

"Oh, right." He smiled. "I often wondered. Well, scratch that theory. There was one about her being a bank robber."

"Right, can you just see my dear old aunt, holding up a bank? Still." She sighed and crossed her arms over her chest as she waited for the total of her purchase. "It does make me wonder. Maybe my parents would know something."

"Wouldn't hurt to ask."

She turned to him. "Obviously you don't know my parents. If they found out I was settling down here…" He watched her shiver and roll her eyes.

"That bad, huh?"

"Let's just say that I'm on radio silence from them until I work up enough courage to tell them."

He put his arm around her and pulled her closer. "Don't let them change your mind. From what I've seen so far, you belong here." He leaned down and kissed her lips. It was hard for him to admit it to her, but he didn't want to see her go. Not when everything was going so well between them.

She set up delivery for her new items for early that next week. Since the water heater had to be installed, he called Roy and set it up so he could install it first thing Wednesday morning.

"Since we've knocked off everything on my first list before lunch, how would you feel about letting me buy you lunch, then going with me to look at a new sofa?" She wrapped her arms around his waist. Since she was looking up at him with her sexy blue eyes, he nodded his head and agreed.

They ate at his favorite buffet place, and then he drove them to one of the biggest chain furniture stores. Here, she spent much longer picking out a sofa and love seat. He actually enjoyed this kind of shopping. The kind where he got to sit in different sofas and try them out. She listened to his input about not buying something the dog's hair would stick to.

In the end, she went with a tan microfiber sofa with recliners on each end. Again, the furniture would be delivered later that week.

"So, anything else on your second list?" he asked as they climbed back into the truck.

She pulled out a piece of paper from her purse, causing him to chuckle. She glanced over at him and frowned. "No, that's it for now. I've ordered some stuff online."

"Like?" he asked, pulling out of the parking lot.

"Items for my students." She leaned back and watched the trees go by. "Thanks for coming with me today."

He reached over and took her hand. "I enjoyed it."

"Really? I got the hint that you're not a shopper."

"I liked being with you." He pulled her hand up to his lips and placed a kiss on the back.

He felt her skin warm under his lips and wished he could explore it more. The drive back felt like it was going to take forever.

"I've offered to cook for Savannah and Billy next Friday," she said, causing him to glance at her.

"Good. You'll like Savannah." He chuckled remembering how his best friend's wife used to be.

"What?" Bella asked, turning towards him.

"Oh, nothing." He shook his head, not wanting to scare Bella away from becoming friends with the new and improved Savannah.

"Is there something wrong?" She frowned at him.

"No!" He squeezed her hand. "It's just that…

Savannah has done a lot of growing up in the past year. Since Maggie was born."

"They're having another one."

"What?" He frowned as he asked. "Another kid? They didn't tell me."

Bella sighed and leaned back. "She seemed very nice."

"Oh, she is. But had you run into her two years ago…"

She shrugged her shoulders. "People change. I mean, look at me. Last month there was no way I'd ever thought I would be mucking out stalls and gathering chicken eggs every morning."

"Now look at you." His eyes roamed over her. She was wearing those shorts he really liked. They had lace over the jean material and hugged her just right. Even her cream-colored blouse clung to her curves. "You look happy."

"I am." She took a deep breath. "Who knew that all it took was getting out of the city. So, will you be there next Friday?"

"I wouldn't miss it." He glanced at her. "You can cook, right?"

She laughed and nodded.

***

Bella couldn't remember ever having had such a fun time shopping with a man before. When they drove up to the house, she was trying to figure a way to avoid ending the evening.

"Did you leave the door open?" Corey asked as he parked the truck.

"No." She gasped and leaned forward to see that the screen door and front door stood wide open. "I locked it when we left. Remember?"

"Stay here." He handed her his phone. "Speed-dial Sheriff Miller. I'm going to check it out."

She sat back and held onto his phone as he walked towards the house. The dogs were nowhere to be found. The fact that they weren't jumping at Corey, begging for attention, scared her and had her imagining all sorts of scenarios where they were hurt.

When he disappeared into the house, she searched through his phone and called the sheriff.

"Hey, Corey, what can I do for you?"

"It's Bella Thompson. We just got home and my door is wide open."

"Bella, I'll send someone out there immediately. Tell Corey to stay put, but since you have his phone, that tells me he's already inside. Hang tight."

She hung up with him and held onto his phone tightly. A few seconds went by, and then the two dogs rushed out of the house and started running circles around the truck.

She jumped out and hugged each one, making sure they were okay. When she looked up, Corey was walking towards her with a frown on his lips.

"They were locked in the utility room. Nothing looks like it's missing, but you can go through it after the sheriff gets here."

She turned and watched the dogs race off to relieve themselves.

"They must have been locked up for a while." She nodded towards the pair.

"Yeah, they scratched the back of the door pretty bad. We might have to replace it."

It took less than five minutes for a police cruiser to pull into the driveway.

"Corey." A dark-haired man got out and shook his hand. "Miss Thompson. I'm Deputy Tanner. You can call me Wes."

"Hi." She shook his hand.

She stood back and listened as Corey explained the situation. Wes disappeared into the house alone with his hand resting on his gun. About ten long minutes later, he walked out again.

"The place is empty. Nothing looks like it's missing, but you might want to walk through it and check."

"What about the cats?" she asked.

"They were upstairs in a bedroom. I let them

out," Wes said as he took notes in his notepad.

"I'll take her around and we'll let you know if anything's missing." Corey wrapped his arm around her shoulders.

Wes handed her his card with the incident report number on the back. "If anything comes up missing, or you find anything else, let us know. In the meantime, we'll have a patrol start driving by once in a while. Just to keep an eye on things."

She put his card into her back pocket. "Thanks."

"Don't mention it." He nodded and turned to leave.

"Do you want me to walk through the place with you?" Corey turned to her after the cruiser disappeared down the driveway.

"Of course." She shivered. "I'm not going in there alone."

He wrapped his arms around her and held on. She let herself sink into him and enjoyed the way he felt.

He leaned back and kissed her quickly on the lips. "Are you ready to do this?"

She reached for his hand and then looked towards the house. The dogs were on the front porch, waiting to get back in.

"Yeah." When she walked in, her eyes scanned the entire front room. The kitchen was off to the left and back of the house, but she could see through the bar area to that room. The living room had been one of the only rooms that she'd remembered about her aunt's place.

There was a large stone fireplace that she had sat in front of as a kid. Taking her time, she walked around and opened each cupboard door in the formal dining room and kitchen. Everything was there. Actually, nothing looked out of place at all.

"Why would someone take the time to break in, lock the animals up, and then not steal anything. I mean... the TV alone is worth something." She motioned to the new flat screen, which was the only item her aunt had splurged on.

"I'm not sure," Corey said. He'd been following her around the house as she went.

"You don't think this had anything to do with the hidden money, do you?" She turned to him. They were now up in her bedroom. Still, they hadn't found anything out of place.

"Probably not. I mean, yeah, the whole town gossips about your aunt hiding money, but no one really thought it was true."

"Except you. You found some. Did you ever tell anyone about it?"

He thought about it. "I might have told Billy and Travis. It was so long ago, I can't remember."

"Why now? I mean, the house was empty for a few weeks after my aunt's death."

111

He pulled her close and brushed a strand of curls away from her face. She loved it when his eyes looked deep into hers.

"I'm sure it was just some kids. Obviously they got spooked away since nothing is missing."

She nodded, knowing he was probably right. Still, just the thought of someone else being in the house when she wasn't there made her shiver.

"Easy," he said, running his hands up and down her back. "If you want, I can stick around for a while."

"I'd like that." She stepped back. "How about I cook something for you? I went to the store the other day and stocked up."

"I could eat." He smiled as he took her hand and they started walking back down the stairs.

Corey sat at the bar area and watched her throw together a meal. She loved to cook and couldn't wait until her new stove and appliances arrived. She'd spent several hours the other day re-arranging the kitchen so it flowed better.

She'd found another stash of her aunt's money and had tucked it inside her purse to help pay for the new furniture. She'd even stopped by the local bank and opened a checking account, depositing everything she'd found so far.

She hoped the break-in wasn't about the money, but what else could it be about? It wasn't as if she had any enemies around here. Or for that matter, anywhere. She'd left Austin after being completely ignored by everyone she'd known.

"You're pretty deep in thought," Corey said from his perch at the bar.

"Hmm?" She turned, still stirring the mix for her chicken. "Oh, I was just trying to wrap my head around the break-in."

"Sometimes there isn't an explanation. I still think it was a bunch of kids that heard your aunt had died." He leaned against the counter. "What are you making? It's starting to smell good."

"Chicken Piquant." She turned back to her preparation.

"What's Chicken Piquant?" He leaned up to get a better look.

"A spicy Cajun chicken over white rice." She turned to him. "You do like spicy foods?"

"Most definitely."

"Good." She turned back around.

"How did you learn to cook?" she heard him ask. Turning towards the stove, she flipped the chicken carefully.

"After I moved out on my own, I decided I needed to save some money and eat at home instead of out all the time. My parents still think a good dinner revolves around which restaurant they want to eat at."

113

"Neither of them cook?" he asked.

"No. When I was younger, we had a live-in nanny who did all the cooking. She taught me a little, then I decided to take a few classes in Austin and…" She turned and smiled. "Fell in love with cooking. What about you?"

"I cook out of necessity. I can make some breakfast stuff and I make a mean grilled cheese." She chuckled along with him.

Chapter Nine

Corey found it harder and harder to keep his eyes from wandering over Bella as she cooked. She had a way of moving in the kitchen that had something else heating up.

She kept him entertained as she cooked, talking about her childhood. He was surprised to find out that she'd visited Fairplay several times in her youth. She had another aunt and uncle that lived in New York. They had three boys that were her only cousins. She wasn't close to them since they were a lot younger than she was. The oldest had just graduated school last year and had enrolled in the Marines.

"I wish I had cousins," Corey said, helping her set the table. "My father was an only child like

115

me."

"I often wonder what it would be like being raised in a big family." She set the dish down and he could see her eyes turn soft with her thoughts. "Someone around my age to play with all of the time. Someone who understood my parents and how I was raised."

"I just wanted someone to take the blame for all the stuff I did as a kid," he joked. He was rewarded with one of those really great smiles she had.

"Sit. I'll grab the food. Would you like a beer?"

He looked at her in surprise. "Do you have some?"

"Sure do. I found out a few years back that I'm a beer kind of girl."

"I think I'm in love." He patted his heart a few times with his hands as she laughed and walked back into the kitchen.

He could hear her moving around in the kitchen as he sat down at the table. He looked around and frowned at the thought of someone breaking into her place. The door hadn't been kicked in. No glass windows busted. Nothing. It was as if someone had waltzed in, put the animals up, and just walked around. Then a thought struck him. Ronny. If it was true that the man had been seeing her aunt, maybe he had a key?

Deciding to check on it first chance he could, he thought about telling Bella, but figured he'd better wait until he knew for sure. If it was Ronny, what the heck had he wanted here? Maybe he'd left some clothes or something else that he needed.

"Everything okay?" Bella asked from behind him.

He blinked and tried to clear his mind from the worry he had about the whole incident.

"Yeah, just realized how hungry I am." He took the beers from her and watched her set the platter of chicken down.

"Where you ever a waiter?" he asked as she smoothly set everything down without spilling a thing.

"For two years during school. But don't tell my folks. They would be mortified if they ever found out their daughter worked a job that didn't make at least six digits a year."

"Are they stuck up?" he asked, scooping some food onto his plate.

"Probably more now."

"Now?" He handed her the plate of veggies she'd made.

"Now that my aunt is gone." He waited as she put some food onto her plate. Then she sighed. "Aunt Betty was the only one in my family that didn't conform to their… standards."

"What would those be?" he asked, taking a bite of the chicken. The spices hit him and he moaned

117

with delight.

"Good?" she asked.

"Wonderful," he said, taking another bite. "Best chicken I've had."

She smiled and took a bite of her own chicken. "My family is full of snobs." She looked down at her plate. "They think everyone should have money. Lots of it. We come from big money and in their opinion, should have more of the stuff when we die than we did coming into the world. My aunt had this place." She smiled as she looked around. He could tell she was proud of everything she saw. "I think I was the only one who understood why she chose to live this way. I was always jealous of her freedom here."

"She did enjoy it. It's a great place."

Bella nodded her head and took another bite.

"I'm happy you chose to stay." He reached over and took her hand in his.

"I am too. Once I have my business up and running and have enough students, I'll tell my folks."

"It shouldn't matter what they think. If your aunt could have a wonderful life here, so can you."

She nodded, but he could see a little fear behind her eyes.

After they were done eating, he helped her take the dishes into the kitchen. He stood at the sink and helped her load the dishwasher. Then he took her hips and moved her away from the sink as she tried to wash the pans.

"I'll do that. You cooked, I'll clean." He moved over and placed a kiss on her lips. "It's the least I can do."

"You went shopping with me today." She leaned on the counter and crossed her arms over her chest. "Dinner was my way of saying thanks."

He smiled. "And this is my way of saying thanks for the food." Her eyes moved over him slowly, and he thought of another way he'd like to say thanks. But instead, he turned to the sink and started scrubbing the pans as she watched him.

"Do you like what you do?" she asked as she dried the pans he'd washed.

"I like working for myself." He glanced at her. "Some of it's backbreaking, but it's honest work. Keeps me out of trouble." He smiled. "I've gotten into a lot of that over the years."

"I'll bet you have. Is it true that you car-surfed right through downtown... naked?"

He laughed. "Yeah, those were the days." He sighed and glanced out the window as he remembered the fun.

"I heard it was just a few years ago." She nudged him with her hip.

He laughed. "Yeah, but it was a special

119

occasion."

"Oh?" She turned to him and he set the last pan down to dry. Drying his hands, he dropped the towel on the counter and placed his hands on her hips.

"Yeah, I was trying to win the attentions of a particular girl." He smiled and moved closer to her.

"Did it work?" She wrapped her arms around his shoulders.

"Not particularly. Especially after Billy slammed on the brakes and I fell back into the bed of the truck. I had bruises up and down my backside for weeks."

"Serves you right. Didn't anyone ever tell you that you can't capture a woman's heart by making an ass out of yourself?"

He laughed. "How do you catch a woman then?"

She moved closer and he felt his heart speed up. "If a woman has to tell you, then you're not the man for her."

She leaned up and placed her lips on his and he lost all ability to reason. Her body moved against his, soft, supple, perfect. His hands roamed over her back, pulling her tighter against him. Even though her body was plastered to his, he felt the need to get closer. He tugged on her hips until she sat on the edge of the countertop. When her legs wrapped around his hips, he moaned as he pushed his desire against her core. His jeans tightened and he desperately wished to rid them both of their clothes as quickly as possible.

His fingers pushed her shirt up until her skin was exposed. Then he dipped his head and used his mouth over the soft silk of her ribs until his lips brushed against the lace that covered her breasts.

She was moaning, soft little sounds that caused his desire to flare and build. He pushed her silky bra aside and latched onto her tight nipples with his mouth and moaned as he felt her peak for him. Her fingers dug into his hair, holding him tight as he lapped at her skin.

He trailed his mouth down to the buckle of her jeans as she leaned back farther onto the countertop. When he tugged on the clasp, she wiggled and helped him slide each leg down and off until she sat before him in nothing but a matching pair of silk panties and bra.

His eyes roamed over her entire body, appreciating the beauty. Then he leaned down and placed a soft kiss over her belly button. He felt her legs wrap around him once more. This time, he moved until they wrapped around his shoulders as his mouth covered the silk that covered her below.

His fingers lightly played over her until he felt her hips move with each push. His tongue soaked the material hiding her.

When he dipped a finger below, she gasped and

he felt her hold still as his tongue touched her soft sex. She tasted like honey and he leaned in for more. Using his fingers and tongue, he brought her to the edge of a peak. When he dipped one finger into her, she cried out his name and arched back.

He hadn't thought it could get any better than before, but just hearing his name ripped from her lips during an orgasm proved him wrong. She was perfection. Glancing up, he watched her eyes flutter open and knew that he had to go slower. With her, it wasn't just about his needs. Somehow, that realization shocked him enough that he took a step back.

***

Bella realized Corey had left her. When her eyes opened, she saw him standing a few feet away, just looking at her.

She'd never experienced a peak like he'd given her. Nothing had ever ripped through her so quickly or so completely before.

Hoping off the counter, she walked over to him and wrapped her arms around his shoulders.

"Come upstairs with me." She reached for him, only to have him step away again.

"I didn't mean…" He shook his head and she felt her heart sink.

"No." He rushed over to her. "It's not…" He stopped and sighed. "This matters." He looked down at her and she could see in his eyes that he was as affected as she was.

"Then come upstairs," she said again, wrapping her arms around his shoulders.

"I don't want to rush into things. I've always rushed… and it never ended…"

"Corey." She stopped him by placing a finger over his lips. "I've never really been cautious, as far as relationships go, and they've always ended badly. I think we both know that this is different." She pulled him tighter. "If we want this to be different, then it's up to us to make it that way."

She felt him relax next to her. When his hands moved to her hips, she looked up into his eyes and knew that he'd made up his mind.

"Come upstairs with me," she said before placing her lips on his. Then she was being lifted into his arms as he carried her up the stairs. The dogs, thinking it was a game, raced him up the stairs, almost causing him to trip. Laughing together, they entered the bedroom. When he set her down on her feet again, her body slowly moved over his. He was still fully clothed, and her exposed skin tingled where he touched her.

She reached up, keeping her eyes locked with his, and started to undo his buttons slowly. He stood still, his arms and hands locked to his sides as she pulled off his shirt.

"Mmm, I just love these." She ran her fingertips over his muscles. He was lean and tall but covered with long cords that had tan skin stretched tight over every inch of him. She took her time running her hands over him, even circling him and enjoying the view of his back. His jeans hung low on his hips and when she ran her fingers over his lower ribs, he held his breath. Then he hissed it out as she leaned up and nipped at his shoulder with her teeth. Her mouth smoothed over the skin and she ran her mouth lower as her hands reached around to unbuckle his belt and jeans.

His head rolled back, giving her better access to run her hands over his chest and tight stomach. She could tell he was letting her set the pace. Tugging a little, she pulled his jeans down his hips until he stood before her in tight black boxer briefs. The muscles in his legs were strong and when she walked around to his front, she smiled when she noticed how hard he was.

Running her fingers lightly over him, she watched his eyes heat. Still, she was amazed at his restraint.

"You know you're driving me crazy." His voice was low as his hands moved to her shoulders, holding her in front of him.

"I want you to know how you made me feel." She moved closer, then leaned up and placed her lips on his shoulder. Then he hoisted her up once more. Her legs wrapped around his hips as he held her up against his body.

"Have no doubt that I know exactly how you

feel. I've felt that since the moment I saw you leaning into the trunk of your car." His lips fussed with hers as he took a couple steps backwards. They landed on the bed softly, his hands rushing over her body, pulling the remainder of her clothes away. "I want to taste every luscious spot on your body," he said against her skin. "Lap it up then do it all over again." His mouth ran down her neck, sending shivers throughout her body.

When she started to tug at his shorts, he pulled back and kicked them off, then bent down and pulled a condom from his back pocket.

When he came back to her, she wrapped her legs around his hips and kissed him deeper than she had ever kissed before.

She enjoyed feeling him slide into her and moaned at how full he made her feel. Not just physically; as she looked up into his blue eyes, she felt complete. For the first time in her life, she didn't care about anything other than that moment.

He continued to talk to her against her heated skin as they moved together. He talked about how her body felt, how he desired her, and how he felt like he couldn't control himself around her. She agreed with every word he said.

She'd desired him from the moment she'd seen him sitting in the dirt, holding his chin. She'd wanted him from the moment she'd seen him answering the door in nothing but a towel. The first kiss the other night had marked her.

His hand moved up, pulling her leg up to her chest as he moved above her.

"Look at me, Bella," he whispered. "I want to see your eyes cloud when I make you come."

She couldn't have denied him. Not when his voice touched her soul so deeply. She watched his eyes as his fingers touched her soft skin, sending her over the edge. Moments later, she felt him tense and he threw his head back with his release.

Then his body relaxed over hers, covering her from the chilly night air.

"When I can move again, I'll grab the blankets," he said as he buried his face in her hair and neck. She felt him sniff her and sigh.

She rubbed her hands over his back. They were slick from their body heat and as the room cooled, she realized she really wanted a shower. "I know what you mean. I'd kill for a shower."

He rubbed his face in her hair and said something she couldn't quite hear. Then, all of a sudden, he was rolling and taking her with him. She was once more in his arms as he carried her to the bathroom.

"What are you doing?" she asked as he flipped on the bright overhead light.

"I like your idea of a shower. So I figured I'd kill two birds..." He opened the glass shower door and stepped in. "Taking a shower"—he let her body slide down his as his arms wrapped around her—"and making love to you again." His mouth descended to hers.

Chapter Ten

The next day, Corey rushed home to change and get his tools after eating a large breakfast she'd made them. Then he'd stayed busy working around her house. There was a lot on Bella's list that he could do by himself. First thing on his own list had been to switch out the locks on the house with new ones. He'd even replaced the lock on the shed, just in case.

Some of the light switches had been wired wrong and when she turned on the light for the front porch, it only worked half the time. He spent the entire morning fixing what he could as she worked outside with the animals.

When lunch rolled around, she came inside and heated up some soup and put together sandwiches. When they were done eating, they both glanced outside when thunder clashed just above them.

129

"Looks like I'll have to get to the garden tomorrow." She frowned over at him.

"What do you say to playing hooky the rest of the day?" He moved around the table and pulled her up and into his arms. Her lips were intoxicating and he doubted he'd ever get enough of them.

"Soft as rose petals and sweet as honey," he said against her skin.

She pulled back and smiled at him as she wrapped her arms around his shoulders. The rain had started and she could hear it pounding away on the metal roof. "I suppose since we're not going to get cleaning the gutters done today…" She reached up and placed a kiss on his lips, then pushed away and tugged on his hand until he followed her. He stopped short on the stairs, when she stood a step above him. She turned and they were eye to eye.

"The first time I saw you, we were eye to eye. Those sexy heels of yours." He shook his head. "What'll it take to get you back into those?"

She laughed. "If you come back tomorrow and clean my gutters, you might just get lucky." She leaned closer. The kiss seared him. She may not have known it, but he would have followed her anywhere at that moment.

She tugged again on his hand, pulling him up the stairs. Their clothes fell to the floor as they quickly stripped them away.

Finally, when it was skin to skin, he felt steadier. Her breaths sent waves of desire over his skin as she ran that sexy mouth over him. His fingers dug into her hips, holding her close. Then she was pushing him back onto the bed and he willingly went.

She straddled him, and her eyes focused on his. "I'm in charge this time, cowboy." She smiled down at him.

"Yes, ma'am." He felt his mouth go dry when she climbed aboard him. His hands went to her hips, holding her down on his length.

He'd never imagined anything could feel so good. She rolled her head back, her long hair flowing around her shoulders. Then she started to move and his eyes closed with pleasure.

"Hmmm, I love the way you feel inside of me," she hummed.

"Oh, god." He didn't know how much longer he could hold out. Her hips were moving back and forth, up and down, all at the same time. He'd never experienced anything like it before.

"Do you like that?" she asked as she leaned down and ran her mouth over his chin. "I'm rather enjoying it," she purred.

He bucked his hips as he held her down and heard her moan. "Yes," he said, wanting her to feel what he was feeling, the utter lack of control. "Take all of me." He did it again and this time, when she gasped, he rolled over and pinned her under him. "My turn," he growled as he took the reins. Her hips kept moving, so he held her down harder, pulling her hands above her head. His mouth covered her complaints as he used his hips. When he felt her relax, he trailed his mouth down her body slowly. He savored every taste, every touch until he felt he could no longer hold back. When he plunged into her again, this time it was different. This time it was all speed and desire.

There was no room for slowness. He had to take her. Had to reach the end with her. He felt her legs wrap around his hips as she held onto him. Heard and felt the moment she let herself go, then fell with her.

***

He'd always felt prepared for everything that had come his way in life. But nothing could have ever prepared him for the way he felt about Bella.

Over the next few days, they worked together fixing up the house, getting everything ready for her new appliances and furniture. She'd called a company to haul all the old stuff away and donate it to needy families. He would have never thought about doing something like that.

It had been hard, returning to the cabin each night after that first one, but he figured she needed her space. Plus, Dutch had been lonely.

Still, each night he lay in his bed, desperately

wishing she was next to him instead of a hairy dog with stinky breath. By later that next week, he was trying to figure out how to skip working with the Wests. But since he couldn't find a good excuse and knew that he needed to help out with Hellion, he continued to haul himself over to their place bright and early every day.

"Looks like someone had a good weekend," Ryan said as he stepped out of his truck.

"Shut it." Corey smiled over at him as he reached out and shook his hand. They had been joking with him for days. Apparently, it had been going around town since their dinner at Mama's. Everyone knew they were an item now and, so far, all the talk had been positive.

"You know, Ryan, I do believe he has the same goofy look you had when you came into town with Nikki," Reece joked.

"You mean the same look you get when Missy is around?" Ryan pushed his brother into the fence, which lead to an almost minute-long battle as the brothers tried to outdo one another. It only ended because Reece knocked his cast against the fence post and Ryan had quickly looked up to the house to make sure Missy hadn't seen the move.

"Shit, man. You trying to get me in trouble with your wife again?" Ryan straightened his shirt.

"Again?" Corey joked.

"Shut it." Ryan glared at him, causing him to

laugh.

"What are we going to do with this guy?" Corey asked, watching Hellion rush around the corral.

"Beats me," Reece said, stepping up on the bottom rung. "I was sure he would have calmed down by now."

"Maybe he's better for bronc?" Ryan suggested.

"No." Reece shook his head. "He's mean as cuss. I'd hate for him to go after someone like he did Corey."

"Yeah." Corey remembered the scare of running away from the large beast as he chased him over the fence. It had only happened once, but once was enough. "He bites too." He held up his wrist to show them the large bruise.

Ryan chuckled. "Ornery through and through."

"If you gentlemen are through." They heard a voice behind them. When they all turned, Missy was standing behind him, her arms crossed over her chest. "I saw that move, by the way, Ryan." She glared at her brother-in-law. "You're just lucky I don't feel much like yelling this morning." She rubbed her large belly.

"You okay?" Reece asked, hopping down from the fence.

She shook her head as she held her back. "No, I tried to hide it from you, but I've been having contractions…"

"What?" Both of the brothers rushed to her side.

Corey stood back as they yelled at one another as they quickly got Missy into Ryan's truck. Ryan climbed in beside his wife after he'd rushed into the house and grabbed a bag. Neither of them said anything more to him as he stood back and watched the show.

"Looks like we have the day off." He turned to Hellion after the truck disappeared down the lane. Then he had an idea. Opening the gate, he slipped on Hellions reins and started walking with the beast beside him.

***

Bella was out in the garden mid-afternoon, pulling up weeds, when she heard the phone ringing. She raced to answer it, only to have the machine pick it up first. When she heard it was a sales call, she decided they could leave a message, but still, she listened as she got herself a glass of tea.

The man was talking about stocks or investments, something Bella had never dallied in before. The most she knew about investing was her small 401k she had from her last job, which had a couple thousand dollars in it.

She had just gone back out to finish her work in the garden when she heard the dogs start barking. Standing up and stretching her back, she walked around to the side of the house and watched Corey

135

walk up with Hellion following him.

"What are you doing here with that beast?" she asked as she removed her gloves.

He smiled. "Taking a walk."

"Reece's place is more than seven miles down the road." She shook her head. The horse looked tired and thirsty. Walking over, she filled a pail and set it in front of the horse, who quickly dunked his nose in and started drinking.

"That was the idea. Wear him out." He pulled the reins over the horse's head as she stood back.

"You're not going to..." But it was too late. He'd jumped up onto the back of the horse, who looked around like he was in shock that someone would dare try such a move when he was tired.

"Every morning we try and work with him after he's had a good night's rest," Corey said, as he sat on the horse's bare back. "I figured a hike might wear him down to where he wouldn't..." Just then, Hellion took off and flew past the barn. Corey hugged the horse's back, laughing.

She watched him disappear in her field and wondered if she should try and follow them. Looking down at the dogs, who just sat there looking bored, she sighed.

"That man is going to get himself killed." She sighed and started walking in the direction they'd gone.

She'd just rounded the edge of the barn when the pair came back towards her. Corey looked in charge this time. He had a huge smile on and his shoulders were arched back with pride.

"Well, I'll be damned. Looks like I won this round."

He pulled on the reins and Hellion stopped just shy of her. For a moment, she was afraid that he wouldn't obey Corey. Then she saw it in the horse's eyes. He was tired, but she could tell that he absolutely loved acting up.

"He's a troublemaker." She walked towards him, her hand held out with one of the carrots she'd just picked. The horse sniffed it and then snatched it from her open palm. "I bet he gets a kick out of seeing you fly off him."

"And then he bites me to top it all off." He glanced down at his wrist and she noticed the bruise, which appeared to be fading.

"So, the question is... Will you have to wear him out tomorrow as well?" She reached up and scratched the dark horse between his ears. He leaned into her hand and rubbed his face against her shoulder. She chuckled as she almost fell over.

"We'll just have to see." He slid from the horse's back smoothly. When he stood next to her, she shielded her eyes from the sun.

"What do Ryan and Reece think?" she asked, pulling out another small carrot from her pocket.

He shrugged. "They're probably still at the hospital."

"What?" She turned to him, almost dropping the carrot.

"Oh, forgot to tell you. Missy's in labor." He took the carrot from her and gave it to Hellion.

"How wonderful." She smiled. "I'd heard a couple people taking bets on when the baby would be here and what sex it would be."

"Watch, it'll be a boy." He started walking back towards the barn. "Looks like you've made a dent in the garden." He nodded towards the small patch of dirt her aunt had planted everything from tomatoes to watermelons in.

When they got back to the barn, he put Hellion in a stall. "How about some lunch?" he asked, turning to her and pulling her closer. "I'm dying for something, seeing as I just walked over seven miles." He leaned down and placed his lips over hers. "There, that's what I needed." He brushed his lips over hers again. "I've missed being with you the last few nights."

"With everything being delivered, it's been busy around here." She wrapped her arms around his shoulders. She'd taken a whole day and had rearranged the living room with the new furniture. She'd even run down to the little hardware store and grabbed a few buckets of paint to touch up the walls. Then, she'd decided to repaint the kitchen a honey color. It really added warmth to the place. She was beginning to feel like the home was truly hers.

She'd even had a few more visitors. Several women, friends of Alex's, had stopped by, including her sisters, Haley and Lauren. They had all come without their kids, just for an adult visit, which had been wonderful.

Her fridge was still stocked with desserts they had brought. She planned on having some of them when Savannah and Billy arrived later that night.

"You'll be here and ready around six?" she asked him a while later as they ate lunch. They were sitting on the front porch, enjoying the cool breeze that was coming through the trees as they drank ice tea. The dogs were lying at their feet, too tired and hot to race around the yard anymore.

"You can count on it. I'll bring the beer." He leaned over and kissed her. His arm was around her shoulders as they sat on the porch swing. "I'd better get Hellion back home." He stood and stretched. "Maybe he'll let me ride him part of the way back."

She followed him out to the barn and stood back as she watched the duo together. "That horse has something to prove to you." She chuckled when Hellion jerked on the reins. "He wants to lead." She walked over and reached up to the horse, who immediately calmed down and sniffed her hands.

"What he wants is another carrot."

"I've got plenty." She walked over to the bucket near the garden and pulled out a handful of them. When she walked back, Hellion's eyes were glued to her the entire time. "I think these are his weakness." She held another one out for him. He quickly snatched it from her hand.

"You may be right," Corey said. "You keep him occupied, and I'll jump on his back."

She was about to stop him, but he moved too quickly and was on the horse's back before she could say anything. She watched Hellion's eyes heat, but then she held up another carrot and he focused on it, instead of Corey.

"That's it. Focus on the carrots instead." She reached up and rubbed his ears as she gave him a few more. "Here." She handed Corey a handful of carrots. He shoved them in his front pocket and then she stood back as he nudged Hellion's flanks. The horse jolted but settled down by the end of her driveway. The dogs had followed them that far but turned back towards her just as Corey glanced back and yelled over his shoulder. "See you tonight."

He waved and then quickly turned his attention back to the horse when Hellion started taking off again as she laughed.

Chapter Eleven

Corey showed up an hour earlier than Billy and Savannah were due to arrive at Bella's. He had even brought along Dutch, who'd been acting like he was dying to get out of the house for a while.

He had a case of beer tucked under his arm as he let himself into the house with the extra key she'd given him. He could hear the shower running upstairs and smelled something wonderful coming from her new stove.

Dutch had been so happy to see the other dogs that he'd let the three of them out so they wouldn't go too nuts in the house. Putting the beer in the fridge, he decided to head upstairs to check on Bella.

When he opened the bathroom door, he called out to her, but didn't get a response.

Walking over, he opened the glass door, only to

have her spin and scream. "Easy." He chuckled. "It's just me. I called out, but your head must have been under the water."

"Oh my god!" She reached over and slapped at his shoulder. "You just took several years off of my life." She stood there, gloriously naked as warm water dripped over her. Her hand was to her chest as she held herself up against the shower wall.

"Looks like you're clean enough." He flipped off the water and grabbed a towel then reached in and took hold of her hips, pulling her closer.

"I was just getting out," she said as he started running the towel over her body slowly. He enjoyed seeing her wet and took his time drying every inch of her.

When he backed her up to the counter, she leaned back as he ran his hands over her warm skin.

"Corey," she squealed. "We don't have time…" She sighed when his fingers brushed over the soft skin between her legs. "They're going to be here soon."

"Savannah is always late," he said, trailing kisses down her neck. "Besides, how do you expect me to stay away after seeing you like this?" His eyes ran over her again. "Wet, soft, and warm." His mouth found her peaked nipple and rolled his tongue around it, causing her to moan and grab his hair. He loved the way she responded to him. He nudged her back until she was half leaning and half sitting on the countertop. Spreading her legs, he knelt between them and used his mouth on her.

"The sweetest honey I've ever had," he murmured against her wet skin. "It's addictive." He gently pushed a finger into her heat, causing her to groan with pleasure. "Yes, that's it, come for me, Bella," he croaked, trying to keep his own needs at bay.

But then she tossed her head back and arched her back as he felt her pool around him. Standing up, he yanked open his jeans and was inside her as quickly as he could.

The feeling of her wrapping around him sent shivers pulsing through his entire body. How could he have ever known that someone could do this to him? His fingers dug into her soft butt as he pulled her closer. She wrapped those sexy legs around him, holding him tighter as his mouth claimed hers.

His. That was all he could think as he pushed her back up against the wall. Forever.

***

Bella needed another shower. She felt her pulse slow as a drip of sweat rolled down the middle of her back.

"You'd better be right," she warned.

"I'm always right. Except when I'm not." He

smiled. "About what?"

"About Savannah being late," she said, glancing over at the small clock on the wall. There was less than twenty minutes now until her company was due to arrive. She needed to hop in the shower, get ready, and finish making dinner.

"I am." He pulled back and set her on the ground solidly. "I'll leave you alone now." He moved to go, but them came back to her and kissed her one more time. The kiss started out light, but as she wrapped her arms around his shoulders, she could feel her body building with desire again.

Pushing him away, she growled. "Go! You're making it worse." She moved to get into the shower again.

"Worse? Or better?" he joked.

"Both." She laughed as she let the cold water cool her heated skin down. "If you want to be helpful, you can set the table." She glanced at him through her wet hair.

"Anything else?" he asked as he straightened his clothes.

"Not that I can think of yet." She turned off the water and stepped out again.

"I can help dry you off." He made a move closer to her. She held up her hands and laughed.

"Not after what just happened. We don't have time for a repeat of that. Not until later." She watched his eyes heat. "Go!" She shoved him towards the door.

"Fine, but I'll hold you to the later bit," he said as he exited the room.

She got ready in record time, sliding on a long white skirt and topping it off with a burgundy blouse. She pulled on a favorite pair of her aunt's boots to finish the outfit. She piled her hair up and walked into the bedroom to look for some earrings.

She'd glanced through her aunt's jewelry box a few times and remembered seeing a pair of garnet earrings. She didn't know if the jewels were real, but they matched her outfit and looked fabulous on.

When she walked downstairs, she could hear people talking in the kitchen and glanced at her watch. She didn't know what time they had arrived, but she was running fifteen minutes late herself.

"Hello," she said as she stepped into the kitchen.

"Sorry we're late," Savannah said as she walked over and gave her a hug. "It's Billy's fault." She glared playfully over at her husband.

"Actually, it's Maggie's fault. She decided she wanted to wear the green dress instead of the pink one." He hoisted their daughter up on his hip. "She has a thing for frogs." He tapped the frog on the front of her dress.

"I like it," Bella said as she walked over and ran her hand over the little girl's dark curls.

"It smells wonderful in here. And looks even better," Savannah said, looking around. "It's amazing how much you've done in such a short time."

Bella glanced over at Corey and thought the same thing about their relationship. How had it progressed so quickly?

"Thank you," she said, her eyes still on Corey.

"How about I take them in the living room while you finish up in here?" Corey walked over and rubbed his hand over her back. Then he leaned closer and whispered in her ear. "You look beautiful."

She watched everyone head into the living room, except Savannah, who hung around. "Can I help out with anything?"

She shook her head. "No, but you can keep me company." She nodded towards the bar area. Savannah walked over and sat down.

"So, everyone in town is dying to know if you've found the big loot yet?"

"Big loot?" She turned and looked at Savannah as she was getting the roast out of the oven.

"Sure, I mean, at least it's been rumored around town that your aunt hid over a million dollars here."

"A million?" Bella laughed. "My aunt didn't have a million dollars." She turned back to her task, but something kept tugging at the back of her mind. She wouldn't have thought that her aunt would have fifty thousand dollars in cash either. Yet, she'd found close to that already.

"Well, it's just a rumor." Savannah leaned against the counter. "That sure smells good. You'll have to give me the recipe. I'm branching out with my cooking. You know, trying to learn new things. I made grilled salmon the other day for the first time. It turned out... okay." She shrugged her shoulders.

"I'd be happy to show you how to do a wonderful grilled salmon. I have this great rub." She walked over and pulled out the seasoning. "You put this on it and just make sure you don't burn it, and voila." She snapped her fingers.

"I'll have to try it." Savannah set the spice down. "So..." She leaned closer and lowered her voice. "Tell me all about you and Corey."

Bella chuckled and walked over to try and get Savannah's take on her and Corey's relationship.

In the past, she'd made easy friends with women because of a boyfriend. But none of the women had been married with children before.

Still, she found herself holding back throughout the evening. She wasn't sure if Savannah was just being nice to her because her husband was Corey's best friend or if she really enjoyed spending time with Bella.

As they sat around the table enjoying dinner, Bella asked how Billy and Savannah had gotten together. Half an hour later, after hearing their story, Bella began to believe that Savannah was sincere in her actions. Hearing how far the woman had come in the past year really gave Bella hope that maybe her parents wouldn't freak out when they heard she was going to stay in Fairplay.

Deciding it was time face the music, she figured on calling them that evening.

After dinner, Maggie started to fuss and the couple decided to call it an early evening.

"Thank you for such a wonderful meal." Savannah hugged her. "We'll have to meet at Holly's one day for a cup of tea. Maggie enjoys reading time there every Tuesday and Thursday."

"I'd love to meet you there sometime." She brushed a hand over the little girl's head. Maggie instantly laid her tired head on her mother's shoulder. "Thank you for coming."

She stood on the porch and waved as their car drove down her lane.

"I talked to Ronny the other day," Corey said, leaning against the railing as she watched the dogs run around the yard.

"Ronny?" she asked.

"Your aunt's boyfriend."

"Oh!" She nodded her head. "About?"

"Well, it seems he still had a key to the house." She felt her heart kick. "He didn't know you were staying here and had stopped by to get a few of his clothes from the closet."

"What about the animals?"

"Well, that's where it gets weird. He swore they were left running around. He knew Chase and I were checking up on them, so he left them alone."

She turned and leaned against the railing like he was. "So, how did they get locked up then?"

He shrugged his shoulders. "Not sure. I told him we changed out the locks and he assured me he has everything he needed. He apologized profusely. He didn't mean to freak you out. Ronny's a good guy."

"Thanks." She laid her hand on his arm. "For checking into it. It makes me feel better. Maybe the dogs locked themselves in the utility room. Their food is in there. Maybe they were trying to get to it and accidentally shut themselves in."

She thought about the cats and held in a shiver. There was no way they had locked themselves in the bedroom. Not when she was sure she'd left them roaming the house along with the dogs. But, she decided to keep that thought to herself.

"I'm glad you had them over. Billy's been

working extra hard lately and needed a break. Savannah has really been trying to clean up her wild reputation around town. For the most part, everyone is very accepting, but making new friends who don't have misgivings about her past helps."

As he talked, he was running his hands over her shoulders, soothing the stress from them. She could almost hear herself purring as he stroked her skin.

"I enjoyed them both. Maggie is a gem." She smiled, remembering how cute the little girl was.

"Yeah, she's the best thing that could have ever happened to them. Funny, a year ago you would have caught me making fun of them for having a kid and wanting to settle down." She watched him shake his head.

"Oh?" She moved closer, settling her head against his shoulder.

"Yeah, I was determined to live free and wild myself. There was no way I was going to fall into the trap of marriage." He sighed as his eyes ran over the dogs playing in the yard.

She held her breath, not sure what he was saying. She'd planned too many times to settle down. With all the wrong men.

She didn't want to fall into that same old pattern. Not when she had every intention of starting fresh here. She'd run away so many times in the past and knew that this is where she wanted to be ten, twenty years from now. This was her new home and she didn't want to mess it up by once again following her path of destruction and settling down with the first man who comes along.

Corey was a great guy. One of the best she'd ever dated. But she wasn't ready to think about making their relationship permanent. Not yet anyway.

"I know what you mean." She sighed and dropped her arms. "I have a few calls to make tonight." She looked down at her hands, knowing she was blowing him off. She really wanted to deal with her folks. For some reason, the urgency was almost deafening in her head.

His eyes moved over her face and when he saw her determination, he nodded. "Time to break the news to your parents?" When she nodded, he moved closer. "If you need me, you know where I am." He ran his hand over her back slowly. "Thanks for dinner." He leaned in and placed a soft kiss on her lips. Heat spread through her, making her question herself. Her body wanted him to stick around so she could enjoy his touches, but her mind kept telling her that her parents deserved to know where she was and what her plans were.

"Thanks." She stepped back and dropped her hands.

"I can take these guys with me, since it appears they're rowdy right now. You might not want barking in the background of a phone call this important."

She watched the two dogs playing with Dutch and made up her mind quickly. "Thanks again."

"I'll bring them back in the morning." He clapped his hands as he stepped off the porch. "Night and good luck." She watched him walk off, calling the three dogs as he went.

Rascal and Rusty didn't even glance back at her as they chased Dutch through the field towards Corey's cabin.

Taking a few cleansing breaths, she stepped inside and grabbed her cell phone from the kitchen counter.

Chapter Twelve

As Corey walked home, his mind played over and over their last conversation. He'd seen the sad look rush into Bella's eyes when he'd mentioned settling down.

He wasn't trying to spook her. Hell, he wasn't even close to thinking about settling down. Or was he? Opening his mind to the possibilities, he thought about where he wanted to be and who he wanted to be with ten years from now.

He wanted to be here. Looking around, he nodded his head in agreement. Yup, here. This is where he'd always felt like he belonged. Turning, he glanced back at the big house and sighed. He'd dreamed of owning the bigger place since he was a boy and had helped Bella's aunt out one summer.

He'd seen the inside of the house and had fallen in love. Of course, he'd also fallen in love with all of the animals Betty had had around back then. Even the pigs hadn't bothered him.

Actually, he was thinking of getting himself a few. Those and goats. Goats would help clear the brush and he'd heard they were great protectors for chickens since they didn't let anything sneak by them. Goats and geese.

Nodding his head, he continued on his way to the cabin. When he opened the door, the dogs rushed in and started playing with Dutch's new toys. They were fighting over a particular stuffed duck when his phone rang.

Seeing Grant's number on the display, he took a deep breath and answered.

"Hi, Grant."

"Hey, Corey. So, your father's hearing was today."

"Yeah, I was expecting a call." He held his breath.

"Well, seems like the judge wants to try some new medicine. He's not convinced that your dad is beyond medical help. They want to transfer him to Tyler and have him evaluated. Then, there's a chance he might be released to your care. If you're willing to sign for him."

He rubbed his forehead when he felt a headache building.

"Do you think there's any chance of it working?" he asked.

"I'm not sure. I know that some cases…" There was a pause and Corey knew Grant was thinking about Mrs. Nolan. "…medicine wouldn't help. I'm not sure how far your father's case has progressed. Hell, we're not even sure what's wrong with him, at this point."

"Yeah." He sighed. It had been playing on his conscious since they'd hauled him away. What if he just had a medical imbalance? Could he really condemn his dad to a life in some facility if taking pills every day would straighten him out? "Okay, let's have him checked out."

"I thought you'd agree. He'll be moved first thing Monday morning."

He nodded, trying not to think about the costs that would be associated with everything he'd just agreed to.

"Corey, don't worry about it. I'm sure we'll find out what's wrong. Your dad's a good man. He just needs some help."

"Yeah, thanks Grant. Talk to you later." He hung up and walked over to the fridge to pull out a beer.

He desperately wished he could talk to Bella about it, but he knew she was probably fighting her own battles with her folks.

He couldn't imagine having parents who

thought the way her folks did, that money and power were all that life was about.

He remembered how her aunt had been. How she'd loved her animals, her small farm, the people in Fairplay. She'd been the complete opposite of how Bella had described her parents. At this point, he couldn't even imagine Bella having that attitude towards life.

She'd only been in town for a month, but she'd proven that she loved the animals and the outdoors.

Sitting down on the sofa, he watched the dogs wrestle around until he felt his head nodding, then he carried himself back to his bed and fell asleep dreaming of Bella.

***

Bella slammed down her phone and rubbed her neck. How could she be from these people? Rolling her shoulders, she walked around the house, locking up. She was so angry. What did her mother and father think? That she was still a teenager who had to be controlled and told what to do?

Did they really think that demanding she move back to Austin would work? Sure, they had paid for her school, which she'd dropped out of to move here. They had also paid for her apartment and car while she'd been in school.

She'd told them to come get the Mazda, since it

was doing nothing but sitting under a tree at the end of her drive now.

But none of that was good enough. They had warned her to sell her aunt's house and continue back to school within the month, or they would pay her a visit themselves.

This news had caused her to cringe. It had been almost two years since she'd last seen her parents. Two whole holiday seasons and birthdays later with only cards in the mail to show for it. Did they really think that she would jump because they told her to?

Flipping off the bedroom light, she crawled into bed and felt Snubs and Beggar jump up on the bed with her. Just hearing their soft purrs as she pet them helped settle her down.

This was where she belonged. This is why she'd left the city. She sighed as she listened to the crickets outside her bedroom window. There was no way she was letting paradise go. Especially since she wanted to explore her relationship with Corey even further.

It took her a while to finally settle down, but when she did, she fell into a deep sleep and dreamed about Corey.

When she woke, it was still dark out and she had to blink a few times before she figured out why she'd woken up. It was quiet. Too quiet. Not even the crickets were chirping anymore.

She heard a low hiss and rumble and felt around the bed for Snubs. Then her eyes adjusted, and she saw Corey standing at the edge of her bed.

"Oh!" she said, holding her hand over her heart. "You scared me again." He'd scared her once today already and this time, he wasn't going to hear the end of it. She wasn't used to living in a large house by herself and if he made it a pattern to continued scaring her by sneaking up on her, she was going to have to take her key away from him.

She moved to turn on the light, just as Snubs leaped from the bed, landing directly on Corey's face, which sent him falling backwards onto the ground. As he lost his balance, he knocked over the lamp on her nightstand. The loud crash echoed in the dark room.

When he stood again, he jerked Snubs loose and tossed the angry cat across the room, over her bed. Snubs landed with a thump at the base of the opposite wall. That's when Bella realized that the man in her room wasn't Corey.

She opened her mouth to scream, just as the dark figure rushed from the room. When she put her feet down, tiny shards of glass jabbed into her feet, causing her to fall down on her hands and knees.

She cried out and reached up for her cell phone.

She punched Corey's number with shaky fingers as she backed up against the wall. Beggar rushed over to her and sat in her lap.

"Hello?" Corey mumbled.

"Corey, someone's in the house." She practically screamed it. "He was in my bedroom. Snubs attacked him."

"I'll right there. Stay on the phone with me." She heard him moving around. "Can you lock yourself in the bathroom?"

"No, there's glass. I'm cut." She hissed at the shards still stuck in her feet.

"Crawl," he choked. "Get to safety."

"He's run off. I think he's left the house." She held the phone tighter to her ear. "He hurt Snubs. I can't see if he's alright," she cried.

"I'm almost there," he said and she could hear his truck racing up her drive. "Damn drive!" She heard him drop the phone. "Hang on baby!" he said.

She closed her eyes and tried to control her fear. Beggar pushed his face into hers and she had to open her eyes again when she heard her front door slam open.

"Bella!" she heard Corey call out. "Stay where you are."

She rested her head against the wall and waited until she saw Corey appear in the hallway. He'd turned on the lights as he rushed up to her. When her bedroom light flipped on, she gasped at the smeared blood all over her legs and feet.

"Oh!" He rushed over to her, only to have her scream for him to stop. He was barefoot and only wearing boxers.

"No! There's glass," she hissed as she held up her hand.

He stopped and looked around, then took her comforter and tossed it over the glass. When he moved to her, he gently picked her up.

"Are you alright?" he asked as he carried her into the bathroom.

"Is he gone?" she stuttered, her eyes moving everywhere.

"Yeah, the place is empty," he said, gently setting her down on the countertop in the bathroom.

"Snubs." She glanced over to where the cat lay on the floor, not moving.

"I'll go check." He handed her a towel. "I'll call the police."

She held the towel to her bloody knees and closed her eyes as he walked out to check on the cat.

"He's breathing," he called out from the other room. "Looks like he's going to be okay. I'll call Chase after I'm off the phone with the sheriff."

She could hear him talking to the police,

explaining quickly what had happened. Then he hung up and called Chase about Snubs.

"Yeah, they're on their way. Okay, see you in a few minutes." Corey walked back into the bathroom.

She'd started pulling the shards of glass from her feet and legs. When he walked in, she glanced up. His hands were covered in blood.

"Snubs?" she cried out.

"Yeah, I've got him wrapped up in your sheets. Chase is on his way. What about you?" He glanced down at her feet.

"I'm okay, just stay with Snubs." She felt tears streaming down her face. "He saved my life."

Corey walked over to her and wrapped his arms around her.

"You don't happen to have any big sweats I can toss on, do you?"

She leaned back and nodded. "Top drawer. I don't know if they'll fit, but they were Hugh's."

He turned, then stopped at the door and glanced back. "Later, we'll talk about why you still have your ex's clothes."

She sighed and shook her head. "Because I paid for them." She chuckled. "And they were expensive. No other reason."

She could tell he thought about it, and then he

nodded and disappeared back into her room.

Chapter Thirteen

Corey sat on the sofa in another man's sweatpants and T-shirt and felt like hitting something. Bella sat beside him, her feet propped up on his lap as he carefully picked out tiny shards of glass.

Chase had come and gone, taking Snubs with him. He'd said something about getting the cat into surgery, but nothing more. Bella was still crying over the entire situation as she pet Beggar on her lap, holding him tight against her chest.

Wes and Sheriff Stephen Miller had shown up just before Chase had. They had walked through the place, making sure it was empty.

"Found the back door wide open," Wes said when he came back into the living room. "Are you sure you locked it tonight?"

Bella had nodded as she wiped the tears from her face. "I had just gotten off the phone with my parents." He heard her hiccup. "I walked around the place locking up."

"Where are the dogs?" Wes asked, taking a seat across from them.

"My place," Corey said as he carefully pulled another piece of glass from her foot with a pair of tweezers. She hissed and closed her eyes, but didn't jerk her foot away. "I took them over there so she could call her folks. Besides, they wanted to hang out with Dutch for a while."

Wes nodded and pulled out his notepad. "You said you put in new locks since the last... incident?"

"Yeah." He frowned and thought about Ronny. Would the old man do something like this?

"What about my aunt's... What about Ronny?" Bella looked over at him.

"Ronny?" Wes asked, leaning forward on the chair.

Corey sighed. "I doubt it was him, but I suppose you'll have to look into it."

It took him half an hour to explain to Wes his conversation with Ronny and how the man had just needed to grab some of his stuff.

"I'll go check it out and have a talk with

Ronny." Wes stood. "Maybe you should go to the clinic to have your feet looked at."

Bella looked down at her feet. He'd already tried to convince her to let him take her into town. But she'd said she was fine and that she just needed to get the glass out and soak her feet.

"Bella, maybe we should head into town. That way we can check up on Snubs."

He watched her struggle with the decision and then instead of waiting for her answer, he picked her up and carried her towards the front door. "We're going to swing by my place so I can grab some shoes and change first." he said to Wes, who quickly nodded.

"We'll lock up when we're done here." Wes replied back. Corey waved to Sheriff Miller as they walked out.

After stopping to make sure the dogs were okay at his place and putting on his own clothes and shoes, he carried Bella to his truck and tucked a blanket around her. Even though it was still very warm out, he'd seen her shivering and was worried she might be in shock.

"I'm fine, really," she said as he drove towards the clinic.

"I know, but they're better equipped to get all the glass out than I am with a pair of tweezers."

"I don't want to be a bother." She sighed and leaned her head against his shoulder.

165

"Trust me, it's no bother." He wrapped his arm around her and held tight.

"I wonder if Missy's had her baby yet." She held in a yawn as she asked.

"Haven't heard yet. Maybe we can check when we're at the clinic. They would know."

He pulled his truck up to the emergency drop and smiled when a woman came out with a wheelchair.

"Wes called and told us you were on your way." She helped him get Bella into the chair. "You can wait here; we'll call you back when we've got her all cleaned up." She nodded to the waiting area.

After Bella was pushed through the doors, he walked over and stood by the counter. Kimberly was a nighttime clerk whom he'd seen a few years back. She was one of the only women in town that he was still on talking terms with. Maybe it was because she'd been the one to cheat on him, instead of him calling the relationship off. But, she'd ended up marrying the man and now had a kid of her own.

"Hear anything about Missy and Reece?"

"Heard from Nikki about an hour back. It's a boy, Levi Colton West. Seven pounds, six ounces." She smiled and flipped through her phone. "Here's a picture." She handed him her phone and he smiled down at the new family. The baby looked incredibly too small as Reece held him in his arms.

166

He glanced up over the phone. "What time?"

She sighed. "An hour after I predicted." She frowned. "Twelve-thirty-two."

He smiled. "Two minutes after my time spot. I wonder if I'm the closest?"

Kimberly shrugged her shoulders. "Ryan has the board. I'm sure he'll let everyone know tomorrow. So..."—she leaned closer—"what happened out there?"

He leaned his hip against the counter and replayed the entire story, knowing it would get out to everyone in town just as fast as the news of the new West baby would.

***

Bella leaned back in Corey's truck as he drove back to his place. They had stopped by the vet clinic and checked in on Snubs, who, they were told, was resting comfortably after surgery. One of his ribs had pierced his lungs and his hind leg was broken. He would have to stay at the clinic for about a week. After that, he would need to wear a small cast and cone. But he was going to live and he'd saved her life. If it hadn't been for him jumping at the guy... She shivered, remembering the outline of the man standing at the edge of her bed. So close.

"You okay?" Corey asked, reaching over and taking her hand.

"Yeah." She felt better sitting next to him. "Is it

167

okay if we grab Beggar and stay at your place tonight?"

He wrapped his arm around her, and pulled her closer. "How about we grab the dogs and we'll all come over. That way, it's like getting back on a horse." He looked down at her for a moment.

"I suppose you're right. I can't avoid staying there. After all, it's my home." She leaned her head against his shoulder, trying to hide the shiver that ran up her spine. "Did Wes tell you how he got in? Other than the back door?"

Corey shook his head. "He said it didn't look like he'd broken the door or the lock. First thing tomorrow, I'm heading into town and buying a security system for you."

"If the dogs had been there…" She sighed and sat up. "How did he know they weren't? You don't think he's been watching the place?" She shivered again for a new reason.

"Whoa, I think you're jumping too far on that one. It's more likely that he got lucky the dogs were gone."

"Do you think it was the same man? I mean, I know Ronny told you he didn't put the animals up, but someone did."

"No, I'm sure whoever was in the house tonight was just a drifter or a teenager looking for treasure. Everyone in town knows your aunt hid money."

She leaned back as he drove up and parked in

front of his cabin. "I'll be right back with the dogs." She watched him rush into the house and less than five minutes later, the four of them came out.

She was so happy to see the dogs, she almost cried. It was funny; just one night away from them had changed her so much. Now, she didn't think she'd ever be able to sleep again without them at the foot of her bed.

When they drove up, she was surprised to see the deputy car still parked out front. "I'll go check in," Corey said, jumping out of the truck and holding the door open for the three dogs to jump out.

Corey went into the house while the dogs rushed around the yard. The sun was just coming up, so the dogs were happily sniffing around.

When Corey came back out, she was sitting on the front porch swing. Her feet were bandaged and feeling so much better in the soft slippers the clinic had provided for her. They had given her pain pills, but she hadn't taken any yet because they said it would make her drowsy.

"Wes hung around waiting for us. He says they'll up their drive-bys to nightly for the next month."

"That's good." She waved to Wes as he drove off.

Corey walked over and picked her up, holding

her close against his chest. "Let's get you back in bed." He started walking her in, but she stopped him.

"I'd rather hang out down here on the sofa for now. The sun's up and I'm not really that tired."

He looked down at her and after a moment, nodded. "Fine, but you'll take those pills they gave you."

She opened her mouth to argue, but he just raised his eyebrows at her, so she nodded. "I'll need something to eat first."

He smiled. "That I can do." He set her down gently on her new sofa and handed her the remote to the TV. "I'll be just a while." He leaned down and kissed her. She held his head close to hers for a moment, enjoying his lips.

"I was really scared." She held in a sob.

"I know, baby." He moved and sat next to her, holding her while she cried into his shoulder. She hadn't meant to let it all loose and had been surprised that she'd held it in for so long. "I'm here now." He rocked her as she cried. "Let it go."

Finally, after she'd soaked his shirt and she was sure her eyes were puffy and red, she leaned back. "Sorry." She used her shirt to wipe the tears away.

"Don't be." He brushed her cheek with his thumb. "If that had happened to me, I'd be the one crying instead of you."

She laughed and shook her head. "Thanks."

He nodded. "I'll be right back with breakfast. Rest. Watch some cartoons. They always cheer me up." He leaned in and kissed her once more.

She smiled. "I guess some Bugs Bunny couldn't hurt."

"That's the spirit. Oh, here's someone who looks like he needs some love too." He leaned down and picked up Beggar and set the cat on her lap. "He's probably worried about his brother."

She hugged Beggar close as Corey disappeared into the kitchen.

When Corey came back, her head was resting on the sofa pillows, the remote had fallen to the ground, and Beggar was snuggled up next to her while she watched Tom and Jerry.

"Here you go. Scrambled eggs, Corey style." He waited until she sat up and cleared a spot for the plate.

When he set the large plate of eggs, onions, green peppers, and tomatoes in front of her, she felt her stomach growl.

"You're going to share this with me, right?" She looked at the large amount of food and then glanced up at him.

He held up two forks. "As long as there's room on the sofa for me."

She moved over and patted the spot next to her.

"I love Tom and Jerry. I always felt sorry for Tom," he said, scooping up some eggs.

"Tom? Why? He's bigger than Jerry."

"Yeah, but if you watch closely, Tom is always just either trying to take a nap or fall in love. Jerry is the troublemaker. Watch." He motioned with the fork towards the TV.

Sure enough, the next two episodes, Jerry was the instigator. By the time their plate was cleared, and her pills were swallowed with a large glass of orange juice, her head was feeling heavy.

"I don't want to go upstairs," she said, lying back down on the sofa.

"Then you can stay right here."

"Don't leave." She yawned and laid her head down on his lap. "Okay?"

He smiled and ran his fingers through her hair. "I'm not going anywhere."

"Thanks." She closed her eyes and drifted off.

Chapter Fourteen

When Bella woke again, it was dark and she was lying in the bed upstairs. She blinked a few times, feeling something wasn't right. She could feel the cats lying at her feet, and when she went to move, their heavy bodies held her feet in place.

Glancing down, she frowned at the darkness and frantically blinked, trying to focus her eyes. Instead of cats tucked by her feet, there were two large hands holding her ankles down. Kicking out, she tried to sit up, only to have more hands pushing her shoulders to the mattress.

When she opened her mouth to scream, no sound came out. She tried moving her head from side to side, hoping to break free. But even her head was pinned down. Closing her eyes, she cried out for Corey to help her.

"Shhh." She heard his soft voice. "It's just a dream." Then she felt his hands gently rubbing her face. "I'm here."

She closed her mind to the evil that had taken her and opened to the softness Corey was giving.

Slowly, her body woke, and she felt his warmth next to her. She could feel the blanket he'd tossed over her and knew that she was still lying on the sofa with him snuggled behind her. His arms were wrapped around her sides as he trailed his mouth against her neck.

"Come back to me," he whispered next to her ear.

She blinked her eyes open, and the soft light streamed in through the blinds, and she relaxed the rest of the way.

"Are you okay?" he asked when she was fully relaxed in his arms. She nodded. "Bad dream?" She nodded again. "I'm here." He kissed her again.

She felt a tear slide down her face and closed her eyes at the memory of being completely helpless. When his hands moved her, she willingly rolled over until she faced him.

When he saw the tears, he used his fingers to wipe them away. "Was it that bad?" he asked, brushing a kiss across her cheek.

"I couldn't move. He was holding me down."

She felt him sigh and then he pulled her closer.

"What would you say to Dutch and I moving in? Just for a while, until you feel better?" He pulled back and looked down at her.

She thought about it. Thought about how she would ever be able to sleep in the bedroom upstairs again without seeing the shadow a few feet away. But, if Corey was with her…

"I'd like that." She wrapped her arms around him and held on.

At noon, Corey left to make a quick run back to his place to get his things. She sat on the front porch with the dogs and waited for him to return. Her feet were throbbing from the cuts, but she didn't want to take any more of the pills that made her sleepy, so she had swallowed a couple aspirins instead.

She glanced up when she heard the car coming down the drive and smiled when she saw the police cruiser.

"Afternoon." Wes waved at her as he got out. "How are you feeling?" he asked, walking towards her. The three dogs raced around him, begging for attention. He dropped down and gave each a pat.

"Better," she said from her spot on the swing. "I have some tea." She nodded to the pitcher on the table.

"Thanks." He walked over, set his hat down, and started pouring himself a glass. "Is Corey around?" He looked towards the door.

"No, he's getting a few things from the cabin. He's going to stay over here for a while."

"Good," Wes said, leaning against the railing and taking a drink of his tea.

"Have you found out anything?" she questioned.

Wes sighed and shook his head. "Seems like Ronny was working the late shift last night. I talked to his son Chris this morning since Ronny was still at the factory."

"Factory?" she asked.

"He works just outside of town at the plant. He's an engineer out there. Been working there since he was in his teens." They heard another car driving down the driveway.

This time it was Corey's truck that came towards them.

"Well, anyway, it couldn't have been Ronny." Wes stopped and shook Corey's hand as he walked up to the porch. He repeated the information for Corey, who sat next to her, his arm wrapped around her shoulders.

"Do you think it's someone looking for your aunt's money? I mean, the rumor has been going around for years."

"I think I've found all of the money she hid away." She leaned her head against Corey's shoulder, enjoying the safe feeling he provided for her. She didn't want to think about last night, or worry who was breaking into her house. "How did they get in? I mean, you didn't find anything busted."

Wes shook his head. "Best we can tell, they picked the lock on the back door."

"Who could do that? I mean, that doesn't sound like teenagers looking for treasure." She sat up and glanced back at Corey, who was frowning.

"I ran into town and got a security system from the hardware store. It's not the top of the line, but it will do until you can have one professionally installed." Corey brushed his hand down her arm.

"We'll keep up our nightly drive-bys and keep looking. Until then, sounds like you've got four guys to watch over you." Wes smiled down at the three dogs lying at their feet.

Bella smiled up at Corey and nodded. "I feel safer already."

An hour later as she stood in the bathroom, steam from her shower fogging the mirror, she couldn't lie to herself. She was scared to walk into the next room by herself. No matter what she did, every time she closed her eyes, the silhouette of the man popped into her mind.

But Bella wasn't the kind to let her imagination and fear keep her from anything. So she pulled back her shoulders, wrapped a towel around herself tightly, and walked into the next room.

She stopped short and smiled when she saw Corey sitting at the edge of the bed. All three dogs and Beggar were lying on the bed behind him.

"Thought you might like some company up here." He smiled at her as he got up and walked towards her.

"Thanks." She wrapped her arms around his shoulders.

"How are the feet?" He glanced down at the bandages she'd just replaced.

"Sore." She shrugged. "But I'll survive."

"Then, we'll just have to keep you off of them for a while." He leaned down and picked her up, then gently set her on the edge of the bed. "Where do you keep your PJs?"

"Top drawer." She smiled when he opened the drawer and whistled.

"Wow." He turned around, holding up a sexy pair of silk underwear. "I'm a lucky man."

"Those are my underwear silly. The other top drawer." She pointed to the left one.

"Hang on just a moment. I think there might be something worthy in here." He chuckled as he pulled out another sexy pair.

"What can I say. I like shopping at Victoria's Secret."

"Hallelujah." He sighed as he put the underwear back and opened the other drawer and handed her a pink pair of shorts and its matching tank top. "These are just as sexy." She pulled the clothes on. "I can't wait to peel those off you." He moved closer to her, but when she tried to tug him down, he shook his head. "First you need some food, and then we'll play." He picked her up and carried her downstairs. The animals all followed along, almost tripping him on the stairs.

"It smells wonderful," she said, at the bottom of the stairs.

"A couple cans of soup and some toast. I didn't want to leave you alone upstairs too long." He smiled down at her, then walked over and set her at the bar. Then he walked over and scooped soup into a bowl.

They ate their soup with toast and finished the meal off with a piece of apple pie that Haley had dropped off shortly after her husband had visited.

When Corey carried her upstairs again, fear was the farthest thing from her mind. His eyes moved over her slowly as he walked and she could see the promises he was making deep in those blue pools. His desire was as plain as hers was. She knew he wouldn't hold back this time.

***

Corey couldn't stop the shaking he felt. His fingers shook when he brushed her hair away from

Jill Sanders

her face as he laid her down. Her eyes were locked on his, showing him that she wanted him as much as he wanted her.

So many emotions rushed through him. Fear. Joy. Passion. Desire. All day long he'd thought about how close he'd come to losing her. Even thought they had only known each other for a short time, he knew that he didn't want to be without her. Moving into her place was the step he knew he had eventually wanted to take, but the second break-in had given him a push to make it happen sooner. Now, he was right where he wanted to be and she was right where he wanted her.

She was looking up at him, her arm wrapped around his shoulders and at that very moment, he knew he felt differently about her than he'd ever felt about a woman. The realization shocked him, causing him to stop his movement.

"Corey?" Her voice was low and laced with sex. "I want you." He allowed her to pull him down, towards her. The softness of her pink tank top brushed against his arms and he knew there was even more softness underneath the material.

His mind clicked off as his body responded to hers. Then her lips were on his, sending his body into overdrive. His hands moved on their own, brushing her skin, pulling her loose clothing aside until finally she lay under him, totally bare for his viewing.

He hovered over her, perched on his knees as

his eyes took their fill. Roaming over every glorious inch of beautiful skin. She was more than he could have ever imagined. Her long hair flowed around her shoulders, her blue eyes sought his.

"You're so beautiful," he whispered, not wanting to break the spell. When she reached up and tugged his shirt, he leaned back and quickly pulled it over his head and tossed it aside. "I could look at you all night." His finger ran a trail from her chin to her belly button, slowly. Her chest moved and she held a breath as he circled the dip and then moved lower.

Her eyes slid closed as his fingers brushed down the light strip of curls and then parted her lips for his view. "So beautiful," he cooed.

He settled between her legs, spreading her wider as he used his fingers to please her. The slickness of her skin caused his jeans to become so tight they were almost cutting off his circulation.

Stepping back, he tugged them off and grabbed a condom from his pocket. When he came back to her, she was biting her bottom lip as her eyes slowly roamed over him. He felt powerful when she looked at him like that.

When he moved back down to her, their skin touched, sending waves of desire pulsing through him. He wanted to go slow, to show her how he felt, but finally his massive desire won. Next thing he knew, he was moving over her, in her, as her legs pulled him closer and wrapped around his hips.

"More," he growled, not quite understanding what he was searching for. Her body responded to his demands as her mouth moved under his. When he felt her convulse under him, he growled and demanded more from her. Pulling her legs up, he pushed deeper, harder, until he heard her panting under him.

Sweat dripped down his back as he moved over her, enjoying the way her soft body took his harder one in. Her lips were soft yet demanding as he took the kisses deeper. He grabbed her hips, sinking his fingers into the softness there. His lips and mouth moved lower, kissing, sucking, licking everywhere he could.

Her nails dug into his shoulders, mixing just the right amount of pain to go along with his pleasure. When he felt her building, he moved faster, harder until finally she cried out his name, and he followed her and sank into the darkness.

Chapter Fifteen

The next day Bella kept herself busy around the house. Corey had a job to do in town, repairing and painting a porch for an older couple. She'd wished more than anything that he could have stuck around for one more day but knew that he had his own bills to pay, especially after he'd told her about what was happening with his father, who had been moved to Tyler and was currently undergoing tests to figure out what was wrong with him.

She'd asked him if he'd visited him, but he'd just shook his head and changed the subject. She understood not being close to your parents. After all, the conversation with her folks the other night was still playing over in her mind.

She'd had too many arguments with them, and she'd never won any of them. This time, things were different. She'd tried to live the way they had wanted her to and had only ended up friendless and brokenhearted.

Now, she was going to try it her way. The way she'd always dreamed of as a child. She'd pulled out the old box of her letters she'd sent her aunt again and spread them all out on the kitchen table.

She'd reread each card and letter she'd written her aunt. Most of them were thank yous that her mother had forced her to write as a child. But she remembered that she'd always taken extra time writing to her aunt.

Betty had been everything Bella had ever dreamed about: single, beautiful, and doing what she wanted without anyone telling her otherwise. Bella had always loved animals. Maybe that's why she'd been so thankful her mother had signed her up for riding lessons. At first, she'd been upset that it hadn't been volleyball or softball. After all, she'd wanted to join a team sport to help make friends. But, after the first few lessons, she'd found out that animals were far better friends than teenage girls who wanted to fight and gossip.

Funny, how one's perspective can change over the years. She'd spent several hours with the women in Fairplay and not once had thought of any of them in such a way.

Actually, she and Savannah had been getting

along very well. Billy and Savannah were set to stop by later that night for a visit. Everyone in town had heard about the break-in and wanted to stop by to check in on her.

Already that morning, Lauren had stopped by and dropped of a coffee cake. She glanced over and decided she could use another piece as she went through the box from her aunt.

When she hobbled back over to the table and set the plate down, she accidentally tipped over the box. Now, letters were everywhere on the floor. Beggar walked over and immediately lay on as many of them as he could.

She laughed and pushed the cat aside as she picked them up. Then she noticed an unopened white envelope that didn't look like it belonged.

Sitting everything back on the table, she looked at the envelope. *Bella* was written on the top in her aunt's handwriting.

With shaky hands, she opened the envelope and pulled out the letter..

My dearest niece,

I know you're probably wondering why I have chosen you to inherit all of my possessions. The answer is simple. I have always been able to see a lot of me in you.

You have always been trapped in a world you don't desire. A world where money and power rule and family and bonding with someone take the back burner. I lived my youth much like you have. Trying to please parents that wouldn't and could never understand, yet alone love me for who I wanted to be.

I hope you will look at my last gift to you as a new beginning. A way to change your life into something you want it to be. I understand the burdens that come with everyday life and have secretly spent years building up my wealth, but have not let it change me or showed others the riches I possess.

My last gift to you, Bella, is your chance at freedom. These numbers will be your guide. 12-26-4-22. You'll need them along with the papers in...

But the rest of the page was blank. Bella must have read the letter a dozen times. She didn't know what the numbers meant or why her aunts letter cut off without the key information. After all, her aunt didn't have a safe or a safety box that she knew of.

She'd searched through her aunts paperwork in her desk, and so far she hadn't found anything that could be a clue with the numbers. But, she decided to have another look when she could.

Then again, Bella hadn't even read her aunt's will. Her parents had only informed her that her aunt had left everything to her.

Did they have a copy? Was there a clue as to what these numbers were in her will? Who would even know?

She tucked that letter into her purse then shoved all the other letters back into the box. The numbers, she could easily remember. They were her aunt's birthday, followed by her own.

She remembered her aunt's birthday only because she had always sent her birthday cards along with Christmas cards every year.

She tucked the box back into the pantry and decided to make a nice dinner for her guests, just to prove that she was feeling okay. Plus, cooking always gave her a sense of empowerment, which she could use a dose of right now.

She took her time deciding what she wanted to cook. Making sure she had everything she wanted, she pulled out potatoes for her favorite Greek potatoes recipe, then some broccoli for her oven-roasted broccoli, and last, she decided to use the fresh cod she had bought from the market the other day. She had found a lemon cod recipe in her aunt's cookbook and decided she would try it out.

She busied herself over the next hour preparing everything, which she found was a little more difficult when you had to sit down during most of it. By the time everything was almost ready, her feet were throbbing. Glancing at her clock, she realized she had just enough time to run upstairs and change before Corey was expected to be home.

She had just gotten out of the shower when the phone rang. Since it wasn't her cell phone, she decided to let the machine take it. Once again, the same man left a message to her aunt about investing her money. Bella found it funny that the man was being so persistent, especially since her aunt wasn't the kind of woman to even have a bank account, let alone put a chunk of her money into the stock market. Deciding to ignore the call, she walked into the bedroom and chose a simple cotton dress to wear for the night. It flowed around her calves and would allow her to still wear the soft slip-on shoes she'd been wearing all day.

When she came back down the stairs, the dogs barked, signaling that Corey was home. The thought of Corey and home stopped her for a moment. So much had happened so quickly, yet she felt like she knew Corey better than anyone else she'd ever been with. Even Hugh, whom she'd been engaged to for almost a year.

"Something smells good in here," Corey said from the doorway, causing her to jump out of her thoughts.

"It should be ready soon," she called out to him.

"I'm going to head up and change," he said from the doorway of the kitchen. When she turned, she held in a laugh.

"What happened to you?" He was almost completely covered in purple paint. He'd removed his boots at the door and had even taken off his socks and rolled up his pant legs.

"Don't ask." He rolled his eyes. "Let's just say, that's the last time I help Mr. Coulter paint his house."

She chuckled and then gasped when she heard another car drive up. "That's probably Savannah and Billy. You'd better hurry." She laughed as he turned and walked out. His backside was covered with even more paint.

"I heard that," he grumbled as he rushed out.

She was just finishing setting the plates when she heard the screen door open.

"Hello," Savannah called out.

"Back here." She smiled as she set down the last plate.

"Oh, look at you." Savannah rushed to her and pulled her into a hug. "Why are you up? You should be sitting down with those legs and feet up in the air." Savannah started tugging her towards a chair.

"I'm fine, really." She stopped her. "Where's the baby?" She glanced over just as Billy stepped in, Maggie on her hip. "Oh!" She smiled. "Look at how cute she looks tonight."

Maggie was wearing a soft pink dress with a matching bow in her hair.

"Froggie!" Maggie started to say, and then tears started pouring from her eyes.

"We seem to have misplaced her stuffed frog."

189

Billy frowned. "I'm sure it's just in the wash, but…" Maggie buried her face into her daddy's shoulder. "Until we find it, this is what we get."

"I might have something…" She smiled. "I left it here when I was six." She made her way towards the stairs. "Make yourselves at home, I'll be right back."

She went into the guest room, opened the closet, and looked around in the boxes she'd just put in there. Pulling out the stuffed alligator, she turned to go, but something stopped her. Two of the boxes she'd taped up and put away last week were open. Setting the stuffed animal down, she pulled the boxes out and looked in them. There was nothing but paperwork in both boxes. She'd labeled them from her aunt's small office desk. She had plans on eventually shredding the material since it was bank statements and utility bills.

Deciding to tell Wes about it, she made her way back downstairs. When she handed the alligator to Maggie, the little girl's eyes got big.

"Louis!" Maggie said over and over.

"Who's Louis?" Bella asked, just as Corey walked down the stairs, freshly showered.

"Maggie loves the Princess and the Frog. Louis is the alligator in the story."

Bella smiled. "If he will fill the spot of Froggie until his return, you're welcome to him."

***

Corey and Billy were sitting out on the front porch after dinner. Savannah was helping Bella do dishes, while Maggie slept on the sofa, still hugging the stuffed alligator.

"So," Billy said, taking another sip of his beer. "Any idea who's breaking in?"

Corey frowned. "No. Wes says that Ronny was working the other night."

"Yeah, I've heard that story. Besides, we've known Ronny our whole lives. He's too old to be sneaking around here at night."

"From the sounds of it, he and Betty did plenty of sneaking around."

"Yeah, but he's not the scary type."

"No." Corey thought about it. He'd thought the exact same thing. Ronny was off the list of suspects.

"Then who? I'm not buying the whole teenage kids theory. You?"

"No." He shook his head and took another sip of beer. "I've been doing some of my own digging. I was helping Mr. Coulter paint his porch today…"

"Yeah," Billy joked. "Everyone heard about that mess. Did you really drop the bucket?"

"Shut up." He growled, remembering where his mind had wandered when he'd lost his footing and dumped the whole bucket of paint on his head.

Billy laughed some more.

"Anyway, before I turned myself purple… who paints their front porch purple anyway…" He shook his head and tried to get back on task. "Before, I was talking to Mr. Coulter, who is the manager for Regional Bank. He was telling me that he thought it had to do with all the money sitting in Betty's bank account."

"Betty didn't keep her money in a bank. Everyone knows that." Billy crossed his arms over his chest.

"Apparently, she opened an account a few years back." Corey added, "At least according to Mr. Coulter."

"What does Bella say about it? I mean, if she inherited everything from her aunt…"

Corey shrugged. "I'm not sure she knows about it."

"Knows about what?" Savannah asked as the two women walked out onto the porch.

Corey watched Savannah walk right into Billy's arms. It was funny—a little over a year ago, he would have never thought that the two of them would make a good pair. Now, he couldn't imagine anyone fitting together better. His eyes moved over to Bella.

"Corey was saying that Mr. Coulter was talking about Betty's bank accounts. How she has a bunch of money in them."

"At the local branch?" Bella frowned as she sat next to him. Corey quickly put his arm around her shoulders.

"That's what he was saying. Did you get any information on it?"

She shook her head. "No, all my parents told me was that she had left me everything in her will. I guess I don't even know what everything is."

"Grant would know," Savannah added.

"Grant? Why would he?"

"He was your aunt's lawyer," Billy added in. "Everyone knew that. Your aunt didn't like banks, but she liked Grant good enough." Billy smiled.

"We can visit him in the morning," Corey suggested. He watched Bella bite her bottom lip.

"I think whoever broke in last night went through a few boxes of my aunt's paperwork."

"What?" Corey stopped swinging and took her hand.

"I just found them, when I went to get Louis." Bella looked deep into his eyes. "I was going to tell you after dinner."

He nodded. "What makes you think that?"

"Well, I'd moved all of her old paperwork into two boxes and labeled them. Then put them in the spare bedroom closet along with some other things."

"And?" he asked.

"The boxes were opened. The tape is pulled off and the paperwork is a mess instead of neatly in the folders like I'd left them."

"We'll take them into the sheriff's office tomorrow morning, as well." He wrapped his arm around her shoulder tighter. "We'll get to the bottom of this." He leaned in and placed a soft kiss on her head.

She sighed and settled back against his shoulder.

"If you need anything," Savannah said, holding onto Billy, "Let us know. The whole town is sorry for what you're going through. Everyone is trying to figure out who this could be and why."

"Thanks," Bella said, smiling over at her.

Chapter Sixteen

Early the next morning, Corey drove them into town. He'd texted Grant and told him they would be stopping by, but didn't mention why. They had dropped the two boxes off to the sheriff's office early that morning, but before they did, he and Bella had gone through them.

They were both surprised when they noticed there weren't any bank statements from Regional Bank. There was no paperwork mentioning the bank or money, only bills, which were always showed paid by cash.

"I don't know how my aunt could live on a cash basis. I mean, just paying your bills every month by taking cash down to the office..." She sighed. "I guess I'm a woman of ease. I like logging in online and paying everything with credit cards."

"Me too." He reached over and took her hand. "At least when I can." He frowned when he thought of all the bills he was now paying portions of, just to stay on top of them all. Even the odd jobs he was doing weren't making a big dent in the medical bills his father was racking up now.

"Have they heard anything about your dad?" she asked.

"Am I that transparent?" he asked, pulling into the parking spot in front of Grant's office.

"No." she shrugged. "I guess I was thinking the same thing. I mean, I'm worried about you." She tugged on his hand until he turned towards her. "I can see it in your eyes. You're worried."

He nodded and unbuckled her seat belt and his, and pulled her closer. "I'm worried about you more." He brushed a strand of hair and tucked it behind her ear as she smiled at him.

"I'm okay, as long as you're here." She leaned in and kissed him.

***

Bella sat across from Grant, looking over at the man from behind his large cherry desk. He was looking at them with a slight frown on his face.

"They didn't tell you?" he asked again.

She shook her head, not sure of what to say. To be honest, her mind had gone blank when he'd given her the news.

196

"What do you mean she doesn't mention a bank account in her will?" Corey asked, leaning his elbows on his knees.

"I mean, there's no mention of a bank account, stocks, bonds, retirement accounts. Nothing. This doesn't mean she didn't have any. Just that she didn't mentioned them when she wrote this up almost seven years ago. According to the will, everything your aunt had at the time of her death is now yours. If the bank has an account under her name, then everything in it, by law, is yours and will be transferred into your name. I can check with the bank…"

Corey nodded just as Bella answered.

"No, we'll stop by first." She twisted her hands. "Does it say anything else?" She asked. "My aunt gave me some numbers?"

Corey blinked and looked over at her. "Numbers?"

She shook her head. "Later," she whispered.

"They might be access numbers to a bank account, safety box, investment accounts, or even a stock account. Your aunt was a very private person when it came to her money. I'll give you a copy of her will, so you can take it with you. The bank should be able to use this as proof for any accounts they have opened for her." Grant turned to his computer and punched a few keys and printer sitting behind him began spitting out papers quickly.

They walked across the street to the bank, and as they were standing in line, Corey talked to a few people he knew, making sure to introduce her to them.

She was so focused on trying to figure her aunt's puzzle out, that she wasn't really paying attention.

Finally, when it was their turn, she stepped forward and explained everything.

"Mr. Coulter will have to see you. You can have a seat and he'll be right with you," the young man said from behind the thick glass.

Corey took her hand as they walked over to the chairs that lined the side wall. "Mr. Coulter will straighten this all out."

She nodded and tried to take a few cleansing breathes. "Do you really think that someone was trying to get the money from a bank account. I mean, breaking in and taking some papers won't get money from a bank."

He shrugged. "I'm not sure, but maybe he could at least shed some light on part of it."

Bella knew Corey was right. At least she felt like they were finally on the right track. After all, she was pretty sure she'd found most of her aunt's cash stashes. She'd combed the house from top to bottom, inside and out. She was fairly certain there were no more surprises for her to find.

A few minutes later, they walked into Mr. Coulter's office. The man was nothing like she'd pictured. He was older than she'd imagined. She knew that Corey had helped him paint his house, but she had expected him to be much younger. The man sitting across from them now was easily in his late seventies.

"Corey was telling me about your problems out at the house." The older man frowned and shook his head.

"We think it might have to do with something you said to me yesterday. About Betty having a bank account here."

He frowned. "Well, now, after I talked to you yesterday, I thought I'd do some of my own digging. Seems like your aunt opened an account with us five years back. She didn't make any physical deposits, but had a lot of money moving in and out of it from a few different places."

"Bella has a copy of her will, if you need proof that she is the…" Corey started to say.

"No, I've got a copy. Grant's office faxed it over a few minutes before you stepped in." He smiled. "That man is sure good at his job."

"Okay." Corey nodded.

"Here's your aunt's account summary. She made a few transfers just before she passed."

"Transfers?" Corey asked.

"Sure, the information is all in that stack of papers." He nodded to the statements he handed Bella.

Bella looked over the paperwork. There was a healthy chunk currently in the bank, at least half of what she'd found in cash around the house, which was now sitting safely in a checking account of her own at the same bank. There were a few larger deposits a few months ago and a couple bigger transfers, all with just account numbers on them.

"What are these account numbers? Can we find out where this money was transferred to?"

"I'm afraid I don't know much more. Just what is there. You can contact the bank it was transferred to for more information. I'm sure they will need a copy of your aunt's will and death certificate to give you more information."

"Mr. Coulter, is there any possibility of someone removing funds from this account. Someone other than my aunt or myself?"

He thought about it. "No, not that I'm aware. We have an online banking system, but our security is pretty tight. Besides, no one has touched your aunt's money since the week before she passed."

The room was silent for a while. "Can I have instructions on how to log in to her account?"

"You won't need any. I can transfer your aunt's funds into the checking account you opened with us two weeks ago. All I need is a signature." He passed over a piece of paper. "I'm good at my job too." The older man winked at her.

As they drove back to the house, Bella was glued to the paperwork in front of her.

"I guess I just don't understand any of this." Corey glanced at the paperwork and frowned. "No, I mean, the cryptic message from my aunt. The numbers. Why someone would break in and go through paperwork. I mean, don't get me wrong, it's a good sum of money, but nothing like the rumor you say is going around."

"I've done some thinking about that," he said, glancing over at her. "What about your family?"

"My family?" She frowned.

"Sure. I mean, not that they would be the one's breaking in, but what if someone thought that Betty had money because of your family? You did say you came from a wealthy family."

She thought about it. "I doubt anyone would know how wealthy my family was or care. Besides, my aunt gave up her rights to her inheritance when she refused to marry the man my grandfather had ordered her to when she was my age."

"Oh?" he questioned.

She nodded. "Yes, it was one of my favorite tales. Actually, I had thought about doing the same thing with Hugh." She sighed and glanced out the window, remembering how tempted she'd been to tell her family she wasn't going to finish school or marry the man they had wanted her to. But, she'd been too weak back then and, to be honest, too scared.

"Did your parents arrange the whole thing?"

"No, but they arranged the party that we met at. My mother doesn't do anything without ulterior motives. She knew he would be there and that I would find him attractive. Before Hugh broke it off, he told me my parents had hinted for him to propose." She sighed and tried to bring up some of the old hurt, but instead, she could only find relief. She was thankful she'd gone through all the pain and shame. If she hadn't, she wouldn't be where she was now. Glancing over, she smiled at Corey's silhouette. He had a strong profile. His jaw was her favorite thing to look at on him besides his eyes and lips. He was so different than the clean-cut Hugh, who never would have gotten his fingers dirty. Glancing down, she could still see some purple paint under Corey's nails and chuckled.

"What?" He glanced at her.

"You have purple paint under your nails." She pointed to his fingers.

"Kind of looks like I painted them, huh?"

She chuckled again. For some reason, the contrast of his calloused tan hands with purple polish made her laugh. "Purple isn't your color.

You should try pink." She giggled.

"Keep it up." He reached over and took her hand as they turned towards the house.

"And you'll what?" she teased.

But his eyes were locked in front of him and she watched that jaw of his tighten. "Damn it!" He pulled the truck to a stop, spitting dirt up, causing dust to go flying.

She looked forward and gasped.

Her little Miata, which had sat under the tree at the end of her drive for over a month, was totaled. It looked like someone had taken a sledgehammer to it. Glass and plastic was everywhere.

"Stay here." Corey looked over at her. "I'll go check it out and call it in." He jumped from the truck as she rested back against the seat.

Tears stung her eyes. She only had another year of payments on that car and had been planning on selling it to pay for the new asphalt driveway she wanted.

She watched Corey walk around the car as he talked on his cell phone. He was very animated as he explained things. His hand was waving around, and then he glanced down at his watch and frowned. She could tell he was calculating how long they had been gone, so she glanced down and did the same.

They'd only been gone for a little over an hour.

Who could have done this? More important, who knew that they were gone?

Corey came back to the truck and got in.

"Well, they're sending someone to take a report and a tow truck." He turned to her. "I'm real sorry about your car."

She'd wiped the tears away, knowing they wouldn't do any good. "It's okay. I was going to sell it anyway. Now I can use the insurance money to pay for my driveway instead." She tried to smile.

Corey watched her closely and then reached over and pulled her into his arms. When she felt his chest against her cheek, the tears started flowing.

He ran his hands over her hair and held her until she heard a car pull up beside them. "I'll handle this. Here." He leaned over and pulled out a small box of tissue from his glove box.

"Thanks." She watched him get out of the truck and sniffled into a tissue. She had to blink a few times to be able to see Sheriff Miller and Corey standing over her car, talking.

The sheriff pulled out his cell phone and took a bunch of pictures while Corey stood back and filled out some paperwork. Leaning her head back against the headrest, she wondered why someone would break in to her place, steal some paperwork, stand over her and watch her sleep, and then destroy her car.

There just wasn't a pattern to anything. At least none that she was seeing. She'd taken some criminal justice classes in Austin where she'd learned how to get inside the head of a criminal, but nothing had prepared her for this. Nothing. This felt personal.

Her mind played over the last conversation she'd had with Hugh. But why would he look through a box of old paperwork? Crossing him off her list, she moved on to Julie, her ex-best friend, who had been dating one of Hugh's best friends. Julie was a wannabe trophy wife. Bella doubted she had the mind of a criminal, least of all someone who could figure out how to pick a lock.

She went down a list of friend after friend. Even went as far as adding her parents into the mix. When no one added up, she started running a list of everyone she'd met locally.

She didn't know all of them well enough to know if they were a threat, but she decided that she would talk her list over with Corey later that night.

Chapter Seventeen

He only got more frustrated as he answered all the questions, explaining what had happened. So many things upset him as he kept glancing down at her broken car.

At least one thing had been confirmed in his mind—whoever was doing this was dangerous. Corey glanced up and noticed Bella sitting in his truck, her eyes glued straight ahead. At least the crying had stopped. He hated feeling helpless as she cried. He wanted to do something, anything, to make it all stop.

"Any idea who would have done this?" Sheriff Miller asked.

"None." His voice reflected his emotions. "We were only gone about an hour. Which means they were either watching the place or…" He dropped off as he thought of something. "Do me a favor— follow us up to the house." He said this last part after he turned his back towards Bella.

"You think they messed with the house again?"

"I have a hunch. I'm hoping I'm wrong." He shook his head.

"Tell you what, if the house looks okay, why don't you ride with me to your place. We'll check them both out."

"I doubt they'd mess with my place."

"Just in case."

He nodded. "Fine." He started walking back to the truck and then stopped. "I'll tell Bella you want some tea while we wait for the tow truck."

The sheriff nodded. "Sure could use some." He wiped his forehead with his sleeve.

"Is everything okay?" Bella asked when he got in.

"Yeah, the sheriff is going to wait up at the house with us. I offered him some tea."

"Okay," she said, watching her car as they started driving by it.

When they arrived, it was just as he feared. The front door stood open as the dogs raced around the yard.

"Damn it!" He threw the car into gear. "Stay

here." When he looked over at her, he noticed that all of the blood had drained from her face. "Hey." He reached over and took her in his arms. "It's okay." He held her, burying her head into his shoulder.

"What does he want?"

There was a quick knock on the window, causing them both to jump. He let out a breath when he saw the sheriff outside and rolled down the glass.

"Stay put, I'll go check it out," the sheriff said, and then he disappeared through the busted door.

"So much for the new alarm," he growled.

"Are the dogs…" She glanced up and sighed when she saw all three playing in the yard. She glanced towards the house.

"I'm sure Beggar is fine."

"How can you be sure?" She started to move.

"No, stay put. You heard the sheriff. Let him do his job." He pulled her back into his arms.

"Corey, why is this happening? There's no more money. They can't get to the bank account now." She rested back against the seat.

"I'm not sure."

She turned to him. "Did my aunt have any enemies?"

"Everyone loved your aunt. Even my old man

went out of his way to help her out."

She looked over at him, waiting.

"Dad used to come muck out the stalls when she was sick. He helped shoe the horses and occasionally your aunt would pay him back when she had a cow slaughtered by giving him some steak." When her eyebrows shot up, he smiled. "We're a small town; we don't pay for everything with cash."

"If it's not that, then it has to be about me." She sighed. "I've been thinking about—" But her sentence was cut off when the sheriff walked back out.

They both got out of the truck. "Well?" Bella asked.

"The place is a mess. I think it would be best if you took Bella and the animals over to your place for the night. We'll look around and clean everything up." He sighed and put his arm out to stop Bella from rushing into the house.

"I have to see." She glanced up at the sheriff. "I need to see it."

The sheriff looked to Corey, who nodded slowly. Corey reached over and took Bella's hand.

"Together." He waited until her eyes met his. Then she nodded and he followed her into the house.

The sheriff was right. Nothing had been spared.

Not even her new sofa. Its soft cushions were cut open, spilling their white cotton stuffing all over the floor.

The small tables were broken in pieces, and all the books from the shelves were tossed around. Papers and glass filled the floors.

"Beggar?" she called, only to have the cat peek it's head out from a cushion, like it was a game of hide-and-seek. Bella rushed over and picked him up, holding him close to her chest.

"He's okay," Corey said, next to her. "I think the dogs helped." He turned and saw the paw prints in some flour in the kitchen. "They probably thought it was all too fun."

She nodded and started walking upstairs. He followed close behind.

The mattress was turned over, the headboard broken off the frame. Her dresser was lying on its front, the drawers empty.

"I…" She turned and ran right into his arms. "I want to go now."

He held her close and started walking out. "You sit tight in the car, and I'll grab a few things."

She nodded and then climbed up into the truck with Beggar in her arms. When he whistled, the dogs jumped into the back of the truck. As he walked back into the house, two more patrol cars came up the driveway.

Walking back upstairs, he grabbed a bag and tossed some clothes in for the both of them. He didn't know what kind of things she would need from the bathroom, so he tossed most everything into another bag.

"Hey, Corey," Wes said, standing in the doorway. "What a mess." He shook his head.

"Yeah, I'm going to get Bella settled, and then I'll be back over to help clean up."

"Don't worry about it. I talked to my family and Haley is watching the kids so everyone else can come over and clean up. We'll have it done by morning."

Corey nodded, feeling a little overwhelmed. "Thanks."

"Sure, no problem. Travis says that if you want, you're welcome to stay…"

He shook his head, stopping Wes. "No, we're good at my place."

"Okay." Wes looked around and Corey could tell there was something else.

"What?" He sighed, hoping the news wasn't bad.

"It's just, well, the sheriff called and asked us to stop by your place before coming over here."

"Damn it!" He growled. "Not there too."

"No." Wes shook his head. "Your place looked

fine, but I did notice this." He pulled out a piece of paper, in a bag. "Pinned to the front door."

"It should be mine. That bitch doesn't deserve any of it. Stay away from her."

"What the hell does that mean?" He felt like kicking something, then noticed the dresser and shoved his foot towards it, but missed.

"Not sure, but we'll get to the bottom of it. Saw you two walking into the bank today. Anything you should tell us?"

"Nothing much. Betty had a checking account she added money to and transferred money out of. The money that was there Mr. Coulter has already moved to Bella's account. This can't be over that or the money Bella found lying around this place." He looked around again and felt his temper grow.

"Probably not, not all this for just a few grand." He shook his head. "Well, we'll figure it out."

Corey nodded and grabbed the bags. "If you need me, you know where to find me," he said before storming out.

Tossing the bags in the back, he climbed in and peeled out in the dirt as he drove to his place.

"Corey," Bella said when he parked the truck in his driveway.

"Yeah." He turned to her, trying to hide his anger from her.

"I'm sorry." She sniffled.

213

"Don't be. This isn't your fault." His mind flashed to the note as he pulled her back into his arms. Beggar meowed and rubbed his head against his chin.

"Come on, let's get these guys inside."

***

Bella sat on Corey's sofa, watching him move around the small kitchen as he made them dinner.

"I can help you know," she said once more.

"Nope, I've got it. Besides, I'm working off my anger," he said over his shoulder.

She was thankful. Instead of angry, she was just feeling tired and run down. Wes had come over about an hour ago and told them that they hadn't found any new evidence.

"It's ready," Corey said, breaking into her thoughts.

"I have a list," she said, biting her bottom lip.

"A list?" he asked as he set the pan of spaghetti down on the small table.

"Of potential people. All men, because I know what I saw that night and it wasn't a woman standing over me." She shivered.

"Okay." He walked into the kitchen and pulled out a notepad and pencil from a drawer. Then he sat down next to her. "Dish up, then dish out." He smiled.

"First one on my list, which I had previously discounted, but after seeing my car, I've added back, is Hugh." She waited for his response. Corey hadn't told her about the note yet, so he shook his head.

"Doesn't jibe," he said, then filled her in about what it had said.

"Okay." She sighed. "At least we're getting somewhere. So, it is about my inheritance." She leaned in and took a bite of food. "Maybe it's not about the money at all. Maybe it's about the house? The land?"

He thought about it. "The only one that's had an eye on that place is me. I've wanted to live there since I was a kid."

She glanced at him, tilting her head as she looked at him. "It can't be you. You were with me both times." She smiled and reached over to take his hand. "Besides, you would have never harmed Snubs."

"At least we have that." He smiled and squeezed her hand.

"It can't be your father, he's... tied up." She cringed.

"Dad never liked the extra land. He's a simple man and only wants to own an acre at a time. And you're right, he's been busy." He frowned.

"Anyone else you can think of?" she asked after they had finished the dishes and moved into the

215

living room. The television was on mute as the news played on the screen.

Corey's list was short. Very short. Most of the names he had scratched out.

"I'll pass this on to the sheriff and he'll check them out. For now, we stay put." He put his arm over her shoulder.

She sighed and rested back while petting Beggar, who was sitting on her lap. "Snubs is supposed to come home tomorrow."

She couldn't wait to get the cat back and smother him with love. Out of all the animals, she had bonded most with the cat that didn't like anyone, except her.

"I know. We'll drive into town and have breakfast, then get him." His hand moved over her shoulder.

"Maybe we can stop by Holly's. I ran into her the other day and told her I'd swing by sometime." She wanted a chance to look around the bookstore, maybe pick up a few books while she was at it.

He took her hand and placed a kiss on her fingers. "Anything you want." He smiled and those sexy dimples flashed, waking her body up.

"Anything?" She smiled back.

His hands pulled her hips until he was hovering above her on the sofa as his lips covered hers.

Chapter Eighteen

By the next morning, Corey was pretty damn sure of one thing. He was totally and completely in love with Bella.

He'd never felt anything like what he was feeling for her now. They had spent the night in his bed, making love until the sun was almost up, getting a few hours of sleep in between, but never letting go of one another.

She was everything he'd ever dreamed of. Everything. He thought of the years he'd wasted. How all it had taken was one look from her to knock him on his ass.

At this point, he couldn't even imagine spending a night without her in his arms anymore.

He thought of different ways to tell her how he felt as he drove them into town the next morning.

Maybe he'd take her out riding today for a picnic. The horses did need some exercise. They could ride around the lake to one of his favorite spots. There he could simply tell her how he felt.

His shoulders tensed, thinking about the words actually coming from his mouth. When he glanced over at Bella sitting next to him in the truck, she looked at him and smiled. At that moment, he knew that telling her how he felt would be one of the easiest things he'd ever do.

They had gotten a little later start that usual, but they were still early enough to grab two muffins and some coffee at Holly's. They sat in the back booth area by the fireplace and went over his list one more time.

Holly's wasn't packed that morning, since they had missed the morning rush, but there was a group of mothers near the back with their small kids enjoying reading time.

"There's Savannah and Haley." Bella nodded. "I'll just go say hi to them." She moved to get up.

"Tell them hi for me." He reached up, tugging on her arm until she leaned down for a kiss.

"I'll be right back," she hummed.

He watched her walk across the room, her hips swaying with each step. How had he ever gotten along without her?

He grabbed one of the local papers that Holly always had lying around. Today's headlines had been about Bella's car. There was even a picture of the smashed thing on the front page.

He flipped it opened and started reading the story, just to see if anyone had another angle he hadn't thought of.

When he was done, he glanced up to see if Bella was done with her conversation with Haley. It took him a moment to register that Bella was nowhere to be found.

He dropped his paper and walked over to where Haley was sitting near the back of the story group. One of her sons was on her lap, fast asleep, while the other was clapping and listening to the story with the other kids.

"Where is Bella?" he demanded.

Haley glanced up at him with a frown. "I thought she was back with you." She glanced around, while she held her sons.

"No." His eyes moved all around the coffee shop. Still, she wasn't around.

"Maybe she went to get a book. She was talking about wanting one to help learn how to can stuff from her garden," Haley suggested.

He nodded and moved towards the book rows. It took him less than three minutes to confirm that Bella was no longer in the store. He asked everyone if they had seen her, only to have them all shake their heads. He walked quickly out to the truck, but she wasn't there either. Pulling out his phone, he dialed her number and frowned when he heard her ring faintly. Following the sound, he found her purse turned upside down, its contents scattered all over the back alley. Her cell phone was cracked and lying next to it just outside the back door of the bookstore. His heart skipped several beats before he could finally move into action.

***

Bella opened her eyes and blinked a few times. It was too dark to see where she was and she couldn't really remember what had happened. Where was she? Where was Corey?

She tried to move, but her hands were stuck together. Her head felt really heavy as she twisted around. She was sure if there had been any light, she would be seeing swirls right about now.

Reaching up with both hands, she touched a spot on her head that hurt the most. There was a large bump and her fingers came away slick with blood.

She tried to think of the last thing she remembered. All she could come up with was talking to Haley at the bookstore. Closing her eyes, she played the conversation over in her mind.

She'd asked about Haley's boys, Conner and Cooper. Cooper had been asleep in Haley's lap while she'd talked to her. Conner had been sitting with Maggie, Savannah's daughter, listening to the story.

Then, she'd turned to go back to Corey, when…

She gasped. She'd seen a man standing in the book aisle. There had been a window behind him, so she hadn't been able to see his face, only his silhouette. At that moment, she had known it was him.

He'd turned and disappeared down another aisle, and she figured on just turning the corner and getting a glimpse of a face. But, then nothing…

It wasn't as if the bookstore had been empty. Surely someone would have seen a man carrying a woman out of the place. Where was Corey?

She tried to move again, this time using her feet. They too were tied together with something. Lifting her fingers up to her mouth, she tried to free herself. When she realized it was duct tape holding her, she remembered watching a video on how to break free.

Lifting her arms high, she slammed them down quickly on her legs as hard as she could. Feeling the tape budge and break a little, she did it a few more times. It took three tries before her wrists were freed. She couldn't sit up, since she was in a small space. She reached down to release her legs from the tape and realized she was in the trunk of a car. A big car.

After getting her legs loose, she felt around for an escape release only to come up empty. It was too dark to see anything, so she felt around for any tools or items she could use as a defense.

Her bag and cell phone weren't with her. There was nothing in the trunk. Nothing. Not even a spare tire. Then she felt the false floor give under her and realized the spare tire and jack might still be under it.

It took some moving around, but finally she pulled the support up and smiled when her hands wrapped around a tire iron. At least she had something.

She calmed herself back down, resting back to the farthest spot in the trunk to wait. As she did so, the back seat moved just a little.

Turning her body around, she pushed and felt it move again. She wedged herself against the back of the trunk and used her legs to kick the back seats until light streamed in. She kept kicking, sweat dripped into her eyes, her fingers were slick as she held onto the tire iron, just in case.

Finally, after what seemed like an hour of kicking, the seats moved enough that she could wedge herself out. When she did, she was shocked to see the state of the car she was in. There were no windows, and the interior was completely ripped up.

Pulling herself out farther, she finally rushed from the back seat and stood just outside of the demolished car. Glancing around, there were piles of cars surrounding her.

She didn't know which way to run. She didn't even know that Fairplay had a junkyard this big. She started walking slowly, trying to think as she went.

Why would someone have done this? What could they have gained? For some reason, her aunt's letter in her purse came to mind.

The numbers. But she had moved her aunt's money to her checking account and Mr. Coulter had assured her...

Something made her stop moving. Things clicked all of a sudden into place. The two voice mails from the man about stocks, the numbers in her aunt's letter. Then she remembered something Grant had said about investment accounts. She wished she would have paid better attention to the man's messages.

If her aunt had opened a bank account a few years back, which was totally out of character, maybe she had also opened an investment account or started messing around with stocks.

First things first—she needed to get out of the junkyard safely. She didn't know if the man who had done this to her was still around somewhere or if he was gone. Her only thoughts were to get back to Corey. She had so much to say to him. So much she'd been too afraid of before.

Finally, she found the edge of the yard and

frowned at the very tall fence that circled it. She stood along the fence and looked down either way, unable to see where the entrance of the yard was. Deciding to head right, it took her almost ten minutes in the scorching sun to find the locked gate.

The chain that wrapped around the entrance was tight enough that she couldn't squeeze between. She looked for anything to help her climb the fence and decided it would be best to remove her shoes, toss them over, and just start climbing.

She ripped her skirt on the barbed wire at the top but was thankful she didn't hurt herself.

When her feet hit the dirt on the other side, she took a few cleansing breaths and pulled back on her shoes. She didn't know how far out of town she was, but somehow knew she had a long walk ahead of her.

Chapter Nineteen

Corey slammed down his fist on the desk and watched as a jar of pens and pencils tipped over. One by one, they all rolled off the desk and onto the floor.

"I'll let that slide, son," Sheriff Miller warned. "But one more outburst like that and I'll have to put you in a holding cell until you calm down."

"Sheriff," Wes said, shaking his head. "How about I take Corey out with me and drive around? Then I can drop him off at his place until we find something else out."

"I'm not going to sit—"

"You'll do and go where we say. At least until we know something. We don't need you running around town like a chicken with its head cut off." Sheriff Miller crossed his arms over his chest as he

225

leaned back in his chair.

"You're just sitting here!" Corey growled.

"I'm sitting here because you're yelling at me. I could be on the phone organizing the search, but I'm having to deal with a violent and very disrespectful young man."

Corey took a couple deep breaths. The sheriff was right. He was only hindering the search for Bella.

"Fine, I'm with you," he said to Wes and started to walk out of the office. "Keep me updated." He turned back to the sheriff and waited until the older man nodded.

They drove through town slowly, checking almost every street. They ran into other people, who were all out searching for Bella as well. So far there were no updates. No sightings. Nothing. She'd just disappeared without a trace.

The sheriff called Wes over the radio and told them that he'd contacted Bella's parents and they were on the next flight and should be in town early next morning.

Then, just before dark, Wes started to drive him back home. They were less than a mile outside of town, when he spotted someone walking on the side of the highway. The figure was limping and was heading into town.

"Stop!" he screamed and reached for the door handle. He jumped from the moving car as it slowed down. He ran towards the dark figure and had Bella in his arms, holding her tight as she cried.

Corey could hear Wes calling the sheriff behind him. He knew the evening would be full of questions. He pulled back, looking down at her and wanted to tell her how he felt, no more delays, but then he saw the dried blood dripping down her face.

"She's hurt," he called back to Wes as he scooped Bella into his arms.

"Corey, I'm okay," she started to say.

"Shush." He smiled down at her. "This time, no argument. You're going to the clinic."

"I just need some water," she said as he sat back down in the car with her on his lap."

Wes handed her a bottled water, and Corey watched as she opened it and drank it all down.

"I've been walking for hours," she said, resting her head against his shoulder as Wes flipped the car around and started heading back into town.

"What happened?" he asked, brushing her hair away from her face. She was covered in sweat, and her clothes were dirty and sticking to her.

"I... I'm not sure. I woke up in the junkyard in the trunk of a car."

"Junkyard?" Wes asked. When she nodded, he reached for his radio and asked for someone to swing by the junkyard and look around.

"Corey, did you find my purse?" she asked.

He nodded. "Your cell phone screen is busted."

"Was my aunt's letter still there?"

He shrugged. "The sheriff has it all."

"I'll ask," Wes said, and then they sat and listened as he talked to the sheriff.

"It was in a white envelope with my name on it," she supplied.

When the sheriff confirmed that it was gone, she rested her head back.

"Bella?" Corey pulled her chin up. "What's going on?"

"I think this has all been about those numbers."

He waited, but Wes had pulled into the emergency spot at the clinic. "Bella, if you know something, you'd better tell us quickly. Do you know who took you?" Wes asked.

"No, I didn't see his face, but I think he works at the bank or has something to do there. I think my aunt had a stock brokerage account. I received a couple calls from a man about it but thought it was just a sales call."

"Chris," Corey growled. "Get someone over to Ronny's place and have Chris checked out."

"On it," Wes said, picking up the radio again.

"Chris?" Bella shook her head slightly. Then groaned and grabbed her head.

"Ronny's son. He works for a stock brokerage company in Houston," Corey said, lifting Bella from the car and placing her into a wheelchair that was waiting for her. Corey followed Bella into the clinic and once more was told to wait, but this time he followed her back, not wanting to let her out of his sight.

"I didn't know Ronny had a son," she said as she moved up to a bed so they could x-ray her.

"He has two. One moved away to New York. Chris is twenty-two. He was at Mama's when we met Ronny."

Bella nodded slightly. "I guess I didn't really pay attention to him."

"No one really does. The guy's been living off his old man for years."

"We need to take her back for some pictures. You can wait here." The nurse gave him a look that told him he wouldn't get away with following her back to the X-ray room.

"I'll be here when you come back." He leaned down and placed a kiss on her dirty cheek.

"Corey." She stopped the nurse from wheeling her out. "I know this isn't the time or the place, but... I love you." He watched a tear slide down her dirty face. "I just had to tell you. I didn't want to delay..."

He leaned down and placed his lips over hers as he pulled her closer. "I love you too. I was going to tell you in a special way." He shook his head. "I shouldn't have waited."

"No." She smiled up at him and wrapped her arms around his shoulders. "No more waiting." She pulled away as the nurse started taking Bella out of the room.

"I'll bring her right back to you." The nurse smiled over at him as she wheeled Bella out.

***

"I don't know how you made it that far with a concussion." The doctor was looking at her over her chart. "We will be keeping you overnight for the head, and since you're very dehydrated, we'd like to keep a close eye on you."

Bella nodded. Her head was still throbbing, but with her hand safely tucked in Corey's, the pain was dulling. It might have had a lot to do with the pills they had given her, but she liked to think it was all due to him telling her that he loved her.

When the doctor finally left the room, they had just a moment alone before there was another light knock and the door opened to Sheriff Miller and Wes.

"Well?" Corey stood up, still holding her hand in his.

"Chris was at home when we showed up. He seemed irritated we were bothering him, but finally he allowed us in. When we asked if we could look around, he became agitated. Then we started asking him questions about where he was earlier today and he flipped out."

"That's when we spotted your aunt's letter on his desk," Wes broke in.

"After taking him to the station, he confessed to the break-ins and threatening you," the sheriff added.

"Why?" Bella asked as Corey sat down again.

"It seems that a few years back, he convinced your aunt to open a brokerage account with him. She started investing some of the cash she'd left lying around. We found all the brokerage account statements in Chris's room. We'll get them to you when we can. Apparently, a few years back, your aunt invested in some stocks that Corey had told her about. Before she died, she had sold all the stocks for a pretty hefty sum by contacting the brokerage company herself."

"To the tune of a few million," Wes broke in.

Bella gasped and looked over to Corey, who just looked back at her with a slight frown on his lips.

"Anyway, when she died, Chris found out and figured he was due his share," the sheriff finished.

"He also said that he thought his dad should have been the one to get your aunt's place," Wes said, shaking his head. "The guy is acting like a

231

spoiled—"

"Wes," the sheriff warned.

"Sorry, well, he is. Look at all the mess he caused." He nodded towards Bella.

The sheriff sighed and nodded once. "So, we've got him sitting in a cell. His dad is down there, seeing to him. Ronny's a good guy." The sheriff added. "We're confident he knew nothing about all this. He never once thought he was due anything from your aunt. I believe he genuinely loved Betty."

"I agree. That's why his name wasn't on our lists," Corey said, looking at her and waiting until she nodded.

"Thank you sheriff for filling us in." She felt her shoulders relax, knowing that the man responsible was behind bars. "What happens now?"

"Well, we have his computers. He was able to log into your aunt's accounts, but hadn't been able to transfer the money out because of the companies strict policies of adding and changing bank information. We'll have him for the federal crime of hacking into her account. I'm sure there's enough proof on his computer to go to trial."

"Either way, we have his confession and enough proof against him that he'll be locked up for a while," Wes added.

"So, he didn't get into Betty's accounts?" Corey

asked.

"No, apparently there's another security password," Wes answered.

"I'm sure you'll figure it all out. Besides, all you'll have to do is contact the brokerage account," the sheriff added. "Well, we'd better leave you to rest. We have a lot of paperwork to finish. We just wanted to stop by and check in on you and give you the scoop."

"Thank you." Bella smiled and shook the sheriff's hand.

"Anytime." He tipped his hat and the two men left.

"So." Corey turned to her. "Think you can still love me even if you're a millionaire?"

She giggled and shook her head. "I'm not getting my hopes up without all the facts."

He smiled. "You know, wouldn't it just serve your family right, knowing that your aunt chose to live the life she wanted and still out-shined them all?"

Bella smiled and tugged on his arm until he moved close enough for their breaths to mix.

"That is exactly the reason I love you." She wrapped her arms around his shoulders.

"What?" He smiled.

"Because you have a way of looking at things

and seeing through them the way I do." She leaned up and kissed him.

His lips were warm over hers and felt like home. She didn't ever want to let go.

When she heard someone clear their throat, she didn't even flinch until she heard her father's voice and jumped when he said,

"What in the hell is going on?"

Chapter Twenty

It took all of Corey's patience to sit next to Bella and listen to her parents argue with her. He didn't think it was his place to say anything, so he remained silent.

That was until her father started demanding she return to Austin with them. Then he stood up and quickly introduced himself.

"I don't care who you are," her father said. Corey guessed that the man's suit had cost more than Corey's truck. But that didn't make him any less of an ass.

"I'm the man that's going to marry your daughter." He stood his ground and crossed his arms over his chest. He vaguely registered hearing Bella chuckle but was more interested in the shocked look on both of her parent's faces. "Now, if you are done arguing over what your grown daughter should do with her own life, I'll ask you to leave so Bella can rest after the terrible ordeal she's been through today. You did hear that she was kidnapped, locked in the trunk of a car, and had to walk almost seven miles in almost a hundred degrees?" He moved to sit down again, but stopped. "Maybe you're just too selfish to care about what your daughter has been through. Maybe you should think about someone else first, instead of yourselves." He sat down and took her hand in his, not giving her parents any more attention.

"How are you feeling?" he asked her gently. He saw the worried look on her face, knowing her folks were still standing there, glaring at them both. His anger vibrated deep inside, but he tried to release it so Bella wouldn't see it.

"I could use another sip of water." She nodded towards the glass next to him. He reached over, his eyes moving to her parents, until finally, they turned and left without saying another word.

"Here you go." He held the water for her and watched as she took a few sips from the straw. "Better?" he asked when she was done.

She nodded and pushed the glass away. When he set it down, she asked, "Did you really mean what you said?"

He chuckled. "I said a lot of things." He smiled

as he took her hand in his once more.

"About marrying me?" She looked down at their hands.

He felt his mouth go dry. "I didn't mean to blurt it out, but yes. I have every intention of marrying you." He pulled her chin up with his finger, until her blue eyes locked on his. "Bella, will you marry me?" He held his breath.

She blinked a few times, and then slowly she smiled. "I'd love to."

He pulled her close and kissed her. This time when someone cleared their throat at the door, he held up his hand, signaling them to wait as he took his time kissing his fiancée.

"What?" he asked, when the kiss broke, his eyes still on Bella's.

"You have some more visitors," someone said. When Corey turned around, he saw several people standing in the doorway, flowers and balloons in hand.

For the next hour, it seemed the entire town of Fairplay shuffled in and out of the small room. He was kind of happy they did, since he could officially tell everyone they were getting married.

Bella seemed to enjoy the attention for a while, but when he noticed her eyes growing heavy, he tried to get everyone out of her room so she could rest. He turned the lights lower.

"Can you stay?" she asked as she made herself more comfortable.

"Chase is going to take the dogs and cats over to his place for the night and check on the other animals. I'm sticking around unless they haul me out of here." He smiled as he toed off his shoes and crawled into the bed next to her.

"Corey," she said, resting her head against his shoulder.

"Hmmm?" He loved the feeling of holding her close.

"I love you," she whispered.

"I love you right back." He smiled and listened to her slow breathing until he closed his eyes.

The next morning, he was woken up when a nurse walked in once more to take her vitals.

Bella was already awake and appeared to feel much better.

"Bella, you have visitors waiting," the nurse said.

"This early?" she asked, glancing at him as he stood up and stretched.

"They've been waiting for almost an hour. I wanted to make sure you got enough sleep." The nurse smiled and winked at him. "It's your parents," she said as she turned and walked out.

He moved to open the door and go talk to them,

but Bella stopped him.

"No, I'll talk to them. I'm much stronger today." She held her hand out until he walked over and took it. "Why don't you run across the way and get some breakfast at Mama's. I need to have a few moments with them alone. Besides, I'd really like to shower as well." He frowned. "I'll be fine. I've dealt with them for twenty-four years on my own."

He sighed and rolled his shoulders. "Okay, I'll be back in an hour."

Corey walked across the street to Mama's. The place was packed this early in the morning. Everyone was talking about what had happened and he had to listen to some of the questions and rumors running around.

"Is it true that old Betty was a millionaire?" everyone asked.

Some of the more elaborate rumors were that Betty had hidden a million dollars in cash in the old house. Of course, he kept his mouth shut since they weren't even sure the sheriff's information was true, at least not until Bella had a chance to talk to the broker.

When he was done eating his food, Grant and Alex walked in with their two kids. Grant helped Alex get the kids settled and then made his way over to where he was sitting.

"I know you've have a busy week, but when

you have some time, I'd like to talk to you about your dad."

"I have some time now." He glanced towards Alex, who was smiling over at him. "If you do?"

Grant glanced back at his wife, who just nodded. "Okay." He turned back towards him. "It sounds like they might have found out what's wrong with your dad."

His heart skipped. "And?"

"Well, the way they described it to me, and after I did a little research on it, it appears your dad has a chemical imbalance. He's showing signs of anxiety, depression, and paranoid delusions. He really believes he was shooting a bear that day instead of Dutch."

Corey sat up a little. "I didn't know that."

"Neither did I until they put him on some new medication and told him why he was there. He broke down and cried as he asked how Dutch was. Sounds like he really liked the dog."

Corey nodded. "He loves all animals. Which is why I knew it was time to do something drastic."

"Well, they want to keep him up in Tyler for a little longer. You know, to make sure the medicine is working. He's agreed to stay for as long as it will take."

"Sure." Corey thought about it and leaned back.

"He asked about having you visit," Grant said.

Corey's eyes moved over to where Grant's youngest was. Emma started fussing as she looked over towards her daddy.

"Sounds like your family is calling." He chuckled as the little girl threw her head back and started kicking as she cried, "Daddy," over and over.

"Yeah." Grant stood up. "Think about visiting him. I think it will do you both some good."

Corey nodded and shook Grant's hand. "Thanks again."

***

Later that evening, Corey drove them back out to her house. When she walked in, she noticed the empty spot where her new sofa and other furniture had been. Other than that, the place was spotless.

"They had a cleaning service come in," Corey said beside her. "We can go furniture shopping this weekend if you want."

"Willing to do that again this soon, are you?"

He smiled. "With you, anytime."

When they went upstairs, they decided to sleep in the guest room, since the big mattress had been destroyed and removed.

Corey sat next to her. "So, how did it go with your parents?" She knew he'd been dying to ask earlier but had held back until she felt ready to talk.

"Well, they know I'm going to stay here. And that we're getting married." She smiled.

"And?" He took her hand and placed a kiss on her fingers.

"And, they are disappointed in me but have decided to keep their opinions to themselves after today. They did mention that I shouldn't expect anything from them. Financially." She giggled as she leaned her head back against the bed frame. The bed was much smaller, and with three dogs and two cats trying to muscle their way on it, she doubted she would have enough room for the night. But it didn't matter and she wouldn't want it any other way. "I'll call the broker tomorrow." She closed her eyes and felt Corey shift and pull her into his arms. "I have enough in savings and in my account to hold me over for a while. Even if this whole thing is just a rumor."

"We'll figure something out," he said, his voice vibrating in his chest, making her feel warm. "Rest, you need it." He kissed the top of her head. "I'll be here and we'll figure it out tomorrow."

She nodded and felt herself slipping into sleep.

The next morning, Corey woke her up with breakfast in bed. Of course, it was hard to enjoy eating in bed when the animals were all begging for a bite of her bacon.

After showering and dressing, she went downstairs and sat at the bar and made the call.

She kept her phone on speaker, so Corey could hear.

The broker wanted a copy of her aunt's will and death certificate sent over before he could discuss anything with her. She used her laptop and her aunt's scanner to send it over and then waited for the man to call her back.

Less than five minutes later, her phone rang.

"Okay, Miss Thompson, it appears as if everything is in order. If you want, I will send you a new password for your aunt's online account."

She entered the website and log-in information into her browser and waited as her internet crunched. When the screen popped up, she felt her head spin.

"What you should be seeing is your main log-in page. The cash balance is in the top left and any open positions your aunt had are on the next tab."

She listened as he rolled through the screens. But her mind was playing over the cash balance she'd seen on the first page.

"To transfer funds out of this account, you will need to first update your bank information, since I assume your aunt's account has been closed."

"Yes," she confirmed.

"To do that, you will go to the funding tab and click on the update bank information link. Then enter your information."

"That's it?" She blinked. "That's all I have to do to move the money from this account to another?"

"Yes, we try and make our process as simple as possible."

She thought of everything she'd had to go through. How easy it would have been for Chris to take the close to two million sitting in her aunt's accounts if he'd just had the right passwords. She felt her head start to throb and held herself back from yelling at the man that, because of this, she had suffered. But instead, she thanked him and hung up.

"Well," Corey said from beside her, "it's funny."

"What?" She spun around and smiled at him.

"You woke up this morning not knowing if you were going to be able to afford to stay in Fairplay, and now, you're easily one of the richest people in town."

She chuckled. "Don't you mean that we're one of the richest couples in town?" She stood up and laughed as he spun her around in circles.

"I love you," she said over and over again.

"I love you right back." He kissed her until she became breathless.

Epilogue

Bella almost tripped on the long skirt when the newest member of her family decided she wanted to chew on the hem. "Star," she scolded as she reached down and picked up the white fluff ball of a puppy. "Go bug your father." She walked over and opened the door, then set the small dog down and knew that she the she'd find her way downstairs with the rest of the animals.

"Are you ready?" Savannah walked in, her long dress flowing around her very large belly.

"As ready as I'll ever be." Bella took one last look at herself in the mirror. The simple white dress clung to her skin. Its off-the-shoulder lace accented the beautiful neckline. Her aunt's string of pearls hung lower and rested just above her breasts. The matching earrings dangled down. Her long hair was tied up in an intricate bun and braids that wrapped around her head.

Walking over, she plucked the white rose bouquet up and took a deep breath.

Her only wish for the day had been that her aunt could be there to see how happy she was. Her parents chose to avoid what was easily the happiest day of her life. But she knew that everyone who mattered was present.

When she stepped out of the back door into her new beautifully remodeled back yard, she couldn't contain her excitement.

There were over a hundred white chairs, all filled with the people she'd grown to love in the last year. Down the long aisle, standing under an arch of while roses and wisteria, stood Corey, the man of her dreams.

As the doors shut behind her, Corey's father, Martin, stepped up and offered him her arm. She smiled at her soon-to-be father-in-law and easily wrapped her hand through his arm.

"You look beautiful." He leaned over and placed a kiss on her cheek.

"Thank you." She smiled. The man was slowly becoming the father she'd always dreamed of having. Now that he was taking his medicine regularly, his life had stabilized and he was back living in his own home, next door.

"I don't know what you see in that boy of mine," he said, causing several people around them to chuckle.

"Shut up old man and bring me my bride," Corey joked, causing more laughter.

Martin smiled as he shook his head. "Impatient. Isn't he?"

She smiled and nodded. "He's waited long enough. Wouldn't you say?"

Martin nodded, and they started walking down the aisle together.

When they reached the end, Corey shook his father's hand and then took her arm.

"I've waited a lifetime for you," he whispered. "Now that I've caught you, I'm never going to let go," he said, just before he kissed her.

Jill Sanders

Sneak peek at Last Resort
(Book one in the Grayton Series)

She was running for her life. Knowing what she would see if she looked back, she kept her eyes trained forward. She tried to avoid roots or limbs that might trip her up, taking each step as carefully as she could at this speed. Her mind flashed to images of what she'd witnessed minutes before, yet she was oddly clear about what she needed to do for a seven-year-old.

Branches scraped her legs and arms as she ran, and her breath hitched with every step she took. Her ears were straining to hear if she was being chased, but she couldn't hear anything beyond her breathing and her loud heartbeat.

When she couldn't run any longer, she ducked behind a large tree and squatted until she was in a tight ball. She tried to slow her breathing down so she could listen, but it took forever to get her breath under control. She didn't hear the footsteps until a shadow fell a few feet from her.

Wrapping her arms around her knees, she waited for what she knew was coming. She was sure she knew what the outcome of the night would be, so nothing could have prepared her for what happened next.

"Are you all right?" a soft voice asked next to her.

Her head jerked up. Her long, dark, stringy hair

got in her face, so she shoved the strands away with her dirty hands.

She looked up and noticed the angel who stood over her. Everything about the woman was aglow; even the woman's clothes shined in the evening light. Her long blonde hair looked soft, softer than anything Cassandra had ever seen. The woman's hands were stretched out to her, and she could see gold rings on almost every finger.

"Here now, no one is going to hurt you anymore. Come with me, Cassandra. I'll keep you safe." The woman's soft voice almost mesmerized her.

Slipping her little, dirty hand in the woman's larger one, she sighed as she felt her soft, warm skin next to hers. She'd never experienced anything so soft in her life.

"How?" she whispered, looking around just in case. "How do you know my name?"

The woman shook her head. "I'll tell you in the car. Come on, we have to move; they're on their way here now."

Cassandra could hear them now. The sound was almost deafening to her tiny ears as her heart rate spiked. She bolted from her hiding spot and ran beside the woman.

The road, which she'd been told never to go near, was only a few feet from them, yet the limbs were thicker here and they had to fight their way through it. The woman's dress ripped as thorns pulled at it. Cassandra's legs and arms bled as deep scratches appeared on her skin.

Finally, they hit the clearing and the woman pulled open a car door.

"Quick, get in." She rushed around to the driver's door and jumped in.

Cassandra sat in the large front seat, her legs tucked up to her chest, her eyes glued to the trees, waiting, watching.

As they sped off, she sighed and her eyes slid closed for just a moment as she let her guard down. Then she opened them and looked at the woman.

"Who are you? How do you know my name?"

The woman smiled at her and glanced in the rearview mirror.

"My name is Lilly. I'm your caseworker."

Cassandra's eyes were glued to her. "What is that?"

Lilly chuckled. "It's like a guardian angel." She smiled and put her hand over Cassandra's hair. Cassandra flinched away, not knowing what the gesture meant. She'd never been touched so softly before.

"What's a guardian angel?" she asked, sliding towards the door a little more.

"Someone who makes sure that you will never be hurt again."

"How are you going to do that?" Cassandra got up on her knees and looked out the back window of the car, making sure they weren't being followed.

"By taking you somewhere where they can't find you. I know this place"—she smiled, looking down at her—"where kids like you can be safe."

Cassandra doubted there was a place like that. Looking out the window of the car as it traveled quickly down the dark road, she thought that there wasn't anyone out there like her. Especially not someone who had gone through what she had. She knew why she had suffered, why she'd been forced to do things she didn't want to—she was the devil's child. Or so her father and stepmother had told her for as long as she could remember.

Her stepmother, Kimberly, had entered her life when she was two. She didn't remember much from before that, but her father had told her that her mother, whom he described as an angel, had died giving birth to her. She had hoped that Kimberly's arrival would save her from the hell she was living—never leaving a ten-by-ten-foot cell—but she quickly learned that wouldn't be the case. This became very clear when Kimberly beat her that first week for stealing a piece of her bread.

As the car drove down the dark highway, Cassandra fell asleep, her little body tense even in sleep. She woke when they came to a stop.

"Sorry, I have to stop for gas. Would you like something to eat?" Lilly asked gently.

"Yes!" she thought. But she knew better than to answer an adult's question. Looking down at her hands, she shook her head.

"Well, I'm starving." Lilly's voice was so calm, it almost made Cassandra believe she could trust her. "You stay put. Promise me?"

Cassandra glanced at the woman. Her smile was so bright. Her blue eyes looked so kind. If ever there was an angel, Cassandra believed it was her caseworker, Lilly. Nodding her head, she looked back down at her dirty hands.

Lilly got out of the car, shutting the door gently behind her.

Cassandra didn't watch as she pumped gas; she kept her eyes and head down like she'd been taught. But when Lilly walked towards the little gas station, she picked her eyes up and glanced towards the building. After she saw Lilly walk through the doors, she looked around. This was a new place. It wasn't the gas station her father had stopped at. This was someplace she'd never been before. Her eyes got wide as she looked at the bright lights. There were large machines sitting right outside the doors.

Cassandra couldn't read well, so she didn't know what the red and white words said. She'd

253

learned her colors from a book she'd had when she was four. Red was spelled R-E-D. She knew all the colors and often would close her eyes and remember every page of the small cloth book that her stepmother had burned one day when she'd been looking at it instead of sleeping.

When she saw Lilly walking back, she quickly ducked her head back down, looking at her dirty fingers. Then she noticed the dirt on the carpet of the car from her shoes. Jumping down, she quickly picked up the larger pieces and shoved them into her mouth and tried to swallow them.

"Here now," Lilly said, getting into the car. "What are you doing?"

"Nothing." She sat back up and prayed that the woman didn't see the dirt she wasn't quick enough to get.

"What do you have in your mouth?" Lilly asked.

"Nothing," Cassandra said again, looking out the window. Tears were streaming down her face.

"Cassandra, look at me, please." The "please" broke through her defenses, and she looked over at the woman.

"I'm not going to hurt you. No one is going to hurt you again. I promise. Now tell me what you have in your mouth, please."

"Dirt," she blurted out. "I'm sorry. I got dirt in your pretty car. I didn't…" She stopped talking and jumped away when Lilly reached over and touched her hand gently.

"Cassandra, look down here." She pointed to her side of the car. Dirt was all over the floor, even on her clothes. "I'm dirtier than you are, I think." She smiled at her and something shifted in Cassandra's heart.

"You..." She took a deep breath. "You aren't mad at me?"

Lilly shook her head. "No, honey. Now open your door and spit the dirt out. It must taste gross."

Cassandra did as she was asked. She'd learned long ago to always do what grownups told her to.

"Now, I bet this will taste a great deal better." She pulled a white bag between them. "I know it's not good to give children soda, but I think this one time we can make an exception." She pulled out a can that looked just like the machine she'd been looking at earlier.

"What is it?" Cassandra asked and then quickly tucked herself into a ball. She knew better than to ask questions. She must be tired to let her guard slip so much.

"It's okay, honey. You can ask all the questions you want. It's called a Coke. Would you like to try it?"

Cassandra nodded.

"I have a turkey sandwich and some potato

chips here. I bought enough for you, just in case you got hungry. We still have a long way to drive before morning."

Cassandra looked at the sandwich. It was wrapped in a bag, and the chips were her favorite kind. She'd snuck one from Kimberly's large bag once and had gotten a whooping, but it had been worth it.

Lilly took out another sandwich and a bag of potato chips and started eating. Cassandra watched her for a few minutes, and then slowly reached over for the food. She wasn't starved. Her father had seen to it that she'd looked plenty healthy when the police showed up, but she was given only what she needed.

"*Kids don't need to eat much. After all, all you do is sleep and poop*," her father had told her over and over. She always thought there was something wrong with her because she wanted to go outside and play—to run in the dirt road, to jump off the tire hill that was in their front yard, or to just lay in the grass and watch the clouds go by.

She slowly opened the bag and took a bite of the sandwich. It was good. So good, she quickly ate every crumb. When Lilly opened the bag of chips for her, she ate every last one of those. Then she heard a noise she hadn't heard before and jumped.

"Would you like to try this?" Lilly held out the Coke can. Cassandra nodded and took the soda.

She took a sip and her eyes slid closed. The bubbles ticked her nose and made her throat feel funny. She looked over at Lilly. Lilly had a smile on her face. "It's good, huh?"

Lilly opened her own soda and drank from it. "Oh!" Lilly said, making Cassandra jump, spilling a little Coke on her clothes.

"I'm sorry." She started frantically wiping the dark liquid off her dirty clothes.

"Honey, it's okay. Don't worry about it." Lilly smiled at her. "I'm sorry for scaring you. I was just going to give you this." She pulled out a package from the white bag. "They're cupcakes."

There were two circles in a clear package. Cassandra had never seen anything like it. They had white swirly lines across them. Reaching over, Cassandra took them from Lilly's waiting hands.

"Thank you," Cassandra said and sat them on her lap before taking another drink from her soda.

"Well, aren't you going to eat them?" Lilly asked.

"They're awful pretty," Cassandra said.

Lilly laughed. "Yes, I suppose they are. Here, let me help you open the package."

Lilly opened the bag and handed one circle to her. When Cassandra bit into it, the richness sank into every pore of her little body. She felt goose bumps rise on her arms and legs. The little hairs on her entire body stood straight up.

"What is this?" Cassandra asked, a smile on her face for the first time.

"Chocolate," Lilly said, smiling back.

The rest of the car trip, Cassandra looked out the dark window and thought about chocolate. How could she get more? Where would she get more? Was it something everyone had?

Her little mind finally ran out of questions, and she rested her head against the car door again. She woke when the car stopped suddenly. This time, the sun was just rising.

"Here we are," Lilly said in a cheerful voice. "Your new home."

The place was huge. Cassandra looked out the front window and instantly was afraid. It had three stories and was cleaner than anything she'd ever imagined.

"There are four other kids around your age living here now, but others come and go. You'll enjoy it here." Lilly got out of the car after honking the horn several times. She walked around and opened Cassandra's door, smiling the entire time.

Cassandra shrunk herself back into the car seat, holding the empty cupcake package tightly to her chest. She shook her head, no.

"I don't wanna stay here."

Lilly knelt down beside her. "It's okay, honey. No one is going to hurt you here. I promise you."

Shaking her head again, she watched as three boys her age came running out the front door. Their clothes were clean and they had new shoes on their feet. Two had dark hair, one with blue eyes and one with dark brown eyes. The last boy had blond hair like Lilly.

Cassandra didn't know much about boys, but she knew they looked tough, and she didn't want to deal with them. She shook her head from side to side, faster.

"Look, here comes Marissa. She's your age and just arrived here last month."

Cassandra looked over just in time to see a girl around her age walk out the front door. She had a small kitty in her hands and was wearing a white dress and sandals. Her blonde hair was pulled back in short braids.

Cassandra looked at Lilly. "I know they have some chocolate in there and if you don't like it here, you can come home with me. Okay?"

Finally, Cassandra nodded and got out of the car, holding onto Lilly's hand as they walked up the front steps under the watchful eye of the four kids and four adults.

Cassandra didn't pay much attention to the kids since she knew the adults were the ones in charge. There were two women and an older man who looked frail. She knew she could outrun him if she had to. One of the women looked strong and capable; the other looked overweight and older. Cassandra knew that didn't mean she couldn't run fast since Kimberly had been pudgy and fast.

"Hi, everyone, this is Cassey." Lilly looked down and winked at her. Cassandra liked the shorter name; she'd always thought her name was too long and too big for her.

"Hi, Cassey," everyone said together.

"Cassey," Lilly said, smiling down at her, "this is Mr. and Mrs. Grayton. They own this house. And these are their daughters, Julie and Karen. Julie teaches school and will be responsible for you."

"Hello," she said under her breath.

"Hi," Julie said, kneeling down to her. Her hands were tan and she wore a faded pair of jeans and a button-up shirt with flowers on it. Her short brown hair was curly and looked soft like Lilly's. Her brown eyes looked rich and warm like the rest of her. "I've made some pancakes for breakfast. Would you like to come in and have some?"

Cassey looked up to Lilly and when Lilly nodded, she looked at Julie and said, "Yes, please."

Other books by Jill Sanders

The Pride Series
Finding Pride
Discovering Pride
Returning Pride
Lasting Pride
Serving Pride
Red Hot Christmas
My Sweet Valentine
Return To Me
Rescue Me (Coming Soon)

The Secret Series
Secret Seduction
Secret Pleasure
Secret Guardian
Secret Passions
Secret Identity
Secret Sauce

The West Series
Loving Lauren
Taming Alex
Holding Haley
Missy's Moment
Breaking Travis
Roping Ryan
Wild Bride
Corey's Catch

The Grayton Series
Last Resort
Someday Beach
Rip Current
In Too Deep

Swept Away (Coming 2016)

NEW Series
(Coming Soon)
Unlucky In Love
Sweet Resolve

For a complete list of books, visit http://JillSanders.com

This is a work of fiction. Names, characters, places and incidents either are the product of the author's imagination or are used fictitiously, and any resemblance to actual persons, living or dead, business establishments, events or locales is entirely coincidental.

ISBN: 978-1-942896-06-7
Copyright © 2015 Jill Sanders – Grayton Press
Copyeditor: InkDeepEditing.com

About the Author

Jill Sanders is the New York Times and USA Today bestselling author of the Pride Series, Secret Series and West Series romance novels. Having sold over 150,000 books within 6 months of her first release, she continues to lure new readers with her sweet and sexy stories. Her books are available in every English speaking country, audiobook, and are now being translated to different languages.

Born as an identical twin in a large family, she was raised in the Pacific Northwest. She later relocated to Colorado for college and a successful IT career before discovering her talent as a writer. She now makes her home in charming rural Florida where she enjoys the beach, swimming, hiking, wine tasting, and, of course, writing.

Made in the USA
Lexington, KY
12 November 2017